"You need someone to watch your back."

Rachel paused and wished there was a better way to put this. There wasn't. "This person is after us. If we're apart, it'll only make it easier for him."

She could tell that Griff wanted to come up with a good argument for her to stay put. But he couldn't. The safest place for her to be was with him and yet it might not be safe at all.

Griff must have realized there was no time to debate this so he nodded. There wasn't much light in the room. Still, he motioned for her to follow him.

"Stay close and watch our backs. I'm sorry it has to be this way," he added. "And if something goes wrong, just get down as fast as you can. Don't try to return fire or fight off this guy."

"All right," she agreed, but it wasn't something she could promise. No way would she just stand by if someone was trying to kill Griff.

FINGER ON THE TRIGGER

———

USA TODAY Bestselling Author

DELORES FOSSEN

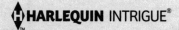

HARLEQUIN INTRIGUE®

Recycling programs
for this product may
not exist in your area.

ISBN-13: 978-1-335-52659-5

Finger on the Trigger

Copyright © 2018 by Delores Fossen

Printed in U.S.A.

www.Harlequin.com

Delores Fossen, a *USA TODAY* bestselling author, has sold over seventy-five novels, with millions of copies of her books in print worldwide. She's received a Booksellers' Best Award and an RT Reviewers' Choice Best Book Award. She was also a finalist for a prestigious RITA® Award. You can contact the author through her website at www.deloresfossen.com.

Books by Delores Fossen

Visit the Author Profile page at Harlequin.com.

CAST OF CHARACTERS

Texas Ranger Griff Morris—This lawman finds himself in the crosshairs of a killer when he tries to protect his mentor's daughter, but Griff could be the very reason a killer is after her.

Rachel McCall—After having a one-night stand with Griff, she left town when she learned he'd kept her father's longtime secret from her. But now she has a killer after her, and Griff might be the only person who can save them both.

Warren McCall—Rachel's father. When his secret affair is revealed, it tears this former sheriff's family apart. But is that affair why his daughter and Griff are in danger?

Marlon Stowe—He has a history of violence, and now he has a vendetta against Rachel because she tried to help his girlfriend get away from him.

Brad Gandy—The district attorney of the ranching town of McCall Canyon. He's also Rachel's ex, and he's not pleased now that she's turned to Griff.

Alma Lawton—She had a thirty-year affair with Warren, but now that he's ended the relationship, Alma might be out for revenge.

Simon Lindley—Alma's attorney and longtime friend. He despises Warren and might do anything to get back at him. That could include trying to kill Warren's daughter.

Chapter One

Something wasn't right.

Rachel McCall was sure of it. Her heartbeat kicked up a notch, and she glanced around Main Street to see what had put the sudden knot in her stomach.

Nothing.

Well, nothing that she could see, anyway. But that didn't help with the knot.

She walked even faster, trying to tamp down her fears. It had been only a month since someone had tried to kill her father and had kidnapped her mother. That wasn't nearly enough time for her to force the images out of her head. The sound of the shot. All that blood. The fear that she might lose both her parents.

There were images and memories of the other things that'd happened over the course of those two days, too.

Remembering that wouldn't help her now, though. She had to get to her car, and then she could drive back to the inn on the edge of town and figure out why this "not right" feeling wouldn't budge.

She continued to walk from the small pharmacy up the street to where she'd parked her car. There had still been plenty of daylight when she'd gone into the pharmacy twenty minutes earlier to wait for her meds to be ready, but now that the storm was breathing down on her, it was dark, and the sidewalks were empty. There were so many alleys and shadows. Enough to cause her nerves to tingle just beneath her skin.

Rachel silently cursed herself for not parking directly in front of the pharmacy, but instead she'd chosen a spot closer to the small grocery store where she'd first picked up some supplies before going for the meds. That grocer was closed now—as was seemingly everything else in the small town of Silver Creek.

She'd chosen this town because in many ways it'd reminded her of home. Of McCall Canyon. But bad things had happened there, and they could also happen here.

The moment her car was in sight, she pressed the button on her key fob. The red brake lights flashed, indicating the door was unlocked, just as a vein of lightning lit up the night sky. A few seconds later, the thunder came, a thick rumbling groan. And it was maybe because of the thunder that she didn't hear the footsteps.

Not until it was too late.

Someone stepped out from one of those dark alleys. She saw only a blur of motion from the corner of her eye before that someone wearing a white cowboy hat pulled her between the two buildings.

The scream bubbled up in her throat, but she didn't manage to make a sound before he slid his hand over her mouth.

It was a man.

Rachel had no trouble figuring that out the moment her back landed against his chest. But she didn't stay there. The surge of adrenaline came. And the fear. She rammed her elbow into the man's stomach, breaking free, and turned to run. She didn't make it far, however, because he cursed and hauled her back to him.

"Shhh. Someone was watching you," he said.

She continued to struggle to get away, until the sound of his voice finally registered in her head. It was one she definitely recognized.

Griff.

Or rather, Texas Ranger Griffin Morris.

How the heck had he found her? And better yet, how fast could she get rid of him?

Rachel pushed his hand away from her mouth and whirled around to face him. She hoped the darkness didn't hide her anger. Even if it did, Griff didn't seem to notice, because his attention was focused across the street.

"Shhh," he repeated, when she started to say something.

Rachel nearly disobeyed him on principle just because she didn't want Griff telling her what to do. But she wasn't stupid. His own expression told her loads. Something was wrong. The knot in her stomach hadn't been a false alarm.

She followed Griff's gaze and tried to pick through the darkness to see if she could figure out what had caused him to grab her like that. There was a row of buildings, mom-and-pop type stores, all one and two stories high. Like the side of the street that Griff and she were on, that one had alleys, too. If someone was hiding there, she couldn't see him.

"Who's watching me?" she whispered. That was just the first of many questions she had for Griff.

He didn't jump to answer, but merely lifted his shoulder. Since he still had his left arm hooked around her waist, she felt his muscles tense. Felt the handgun that he'd drawn, too. Apparently Rachel wasn't the only one who'd thought something was wrong.

"Is this about my father?" she pressed.

That only earned her another shoulder lift. For a couple seconds, anyway. "Your dad's alive, by the way. Just in case you want to know."

She hadn't needed Griff to tell her that. Rachel had kept up with the news about his shooting. Her father had survived the surgery and had been released from the hospital. She hadn't wanted him dead. But Rachel no longer wanted him in her life.

That applied to Griff, too.

"I got here about five minutes ago," Griff went on. He tipped his head toward the end of the street. "I parked up there and came to your car to wait for you. That's when I saw the guy across the street. He's about six feet tall, medium build and dressed all in black. I didn't get a look at his face because he stepped back when he saw me."

Even though Griff and she were at odds—big odds—she believed everything he'd just said. Griff wasn't the sort to make up something like that just to get her in his arms again. Though it had worked. Here she was, right against him. Rachel was about to do something about that, but Griff spoke before she could put a couple inches of space between them.

"Keep watch of the alley behind us," he said. "I don't want him backtracking and sneaking up on us."

That tightened the knot even more, and Rachel wished she'd brought her gun with her. Too bad she'd left it at the inn.

"There might be nothing to this," she whispered. However, she did turn so she could keep an eye on the back alley. "Unless..." She almost hated to finish that. "Has there been another attack? Did someone try to kill my father again?"

Griff didn't answer right away, but he did spare her a glance. He looked down at her just as she looked up at him. Their gazes connected. It was too dark to see the color of his eyes, but she knew they were gunmetal gray.

Rachel also knew the heat was still there.

Good grief. After everything that had happened, it should be gone. Should be as cold as ice. But here it was, just as it always had been. Well, it could take a hike. Her body might still be attracted to Griff, but she'd learned her lesson, and she wouldn't give him another chance to crush her.

"There have been new threats," he finally said. A muscle flickered in his jaw. "Both emails and phone calls. Have you gotten any?"

She shook her head. "No, but then I closed my email account and have been using a burner cell."

Of course Griff knew that, because he was the reason she'd gone to such lengths. Rachel had been trying to get away from him.

"How'd you find me?" she snapped. "*Why* did you find me? Because I made it clear that I didn't want to see you."

There was too much emotion in her voice. Not good. Because it meant she was no longer whispering. Rachel tried to rein in her feelings so she could keep watch and put an end to this visit.

"Your meds," Griff said.

Because she was still doing some emotion-reining, she didn't immediately make the connection. Then Rachel remembered she'd needed the pharmacist to call her former doctor in McCall Canyon to verify the prescription for her epilepsy medicine. Without them, she would have had a seizure, something that hadn't happened in two years.

Rachel cursed herself for that lapse. She should have figured out a way to get the meds without anyone having to contact Dr. Baldwin. Of course, Dr. Baldwin shouldn't have ratted her out to Griff, either, and as soon as she could, she'd have a chat with the man about that.

"I'd been so careful," she mumbled. She hadn't meant to say that aloud, and it got Griff's attention because he glanced at her again.

"No. You haven't been. You shouldn't have parked here. If I could find you, then so could the person who made those new threats."

She couldn't argue with that, but what Rachel could dispute was that the person who'd made those new threats might not even be after her. Yes, a month ago someone had put a bullet in her father's chest while he'd been in the parking lot of the sheriff's office where both her brothers worked. But that person, Whitney Goble, who'd been responsible for the shooting, had tried to kill Rachel's father so Whitney could set up someone else that she wanted to punish. Now, Whitney was dead.

Not that it helped lessen the memories just because Whitney was no longer alive.

No. Because of everything else that'd happened in the twenty-four hours following the shooting. That's when they'd learned that her father also had secrets.

Well, one secret, anyway.

That, too, twisted away at her. Just as much as reading the threat he'd gotten and seeing him gunned down in the parking lot. But the truth was her father had been living two lives and had a mistress and a son living several counties over. Her brothers, Egan and Court, hadn't known. Neither had her mother, Helen.

But Griff had.

Of course, Griff hadn't breathed a word about it. Not after the shooting. Not even when later that night she'd gone to his bed to help ease the worry she was feeling for her father. That's why the cut had felt so deep. Griff had known, and he hadn't told her.

All of those emotions came flooding back. "I don't want you here," she said.

If her words stung, he showed no signs of it. "Yeah,

I got that, but I made a promise to your mother that I'd keep you safe."

It didn't surprise her that her mother had made that request. Or that Griff had carried it out. But there was possibly another side to this. "Are you using this as a way to mend fences with me? Because if so, it won't work."

He didn't even acknowledge that, but Griff did push her behind him. He brought up his gun as if getting ready to fire. That put her heart right in her throat, and Rachel came up on her toes so she could see over Griff's shoulder. She shook her head and was about to tell him she didn't see anything.

But she did.

Rachel saw someone move in the alley to the right of the small hardware store. Since it was only 8:00 p.m., she reminded herself that it could be someone putting out the trash. However, that knot in her stomach returned. It was a feeling that her brothers had always told her never to ignore.

Was this the person who'd made those new threats against her family?

Maybe. Whoever it was definitely seemed to be lurking. And looking in their direction. Rachel doubted the person could see them because Griff and she were deep enough in the shadows on this side of the street. Or at least they would be unless there was more lightning. Which was a strong possibility. She could hear more thunder rumbling in the distance.

"Why would someone want to hurt me?" she whispered.

"To get back at your father. At Warren," Griff answered without hesitation. "Everyone in the McCall family could be at risk. Don't worry," he quickly added. "We have a guard on your mother's room at the hospital."

Good. Because her mother was mentally fragile right now. Suffering from a breakdown. Helen didn't need to be fighting off idiots obsessed with getting back at Warren.

Rachel felt the first drops of rain hit her face. They no doubt hit Griff, too, but they didn't cause him to lose focus. He kept watching the man across the street. But the guy wasn't moving. She did see something, however. The flash of light, maybe from a match or lighter. A moment later, a small red circle of fire winked in and out.

That caused her to breathe a little easier. "He's just smoking."

But Griff didn't budge. "He's carrying a gun."

Rachel certainly hadn't seen anything to indicate that, but she took a closer look. She had to wait several snail-crawling moments, but she finally saw the glint of metal. Maybe a gun in his right hand.

More raindrops came. So did the vein of lightning

that lit up the sky, and Griff automatically moved her deeper into the alley. He also took out his phone.

"I'm calling the locals for backup," he said, without taking his attention off the man. "Yeah, it's me again," he added, speaking to whoever answered.

That probably meant Griff had already been in touch with local law enforcement. In fact, he'd probably called them as soon as he'd figured out she was in Silver Creek.

"Do a quiet approach," Griff instructed. "If you can, try to get someone behind this guy so we can take him into custody." He ended the call and put his phone away.

She doubted it would take long for someone to arrive, but it would feel like an eternity. And might be completely unnecessary.

"If he means to do me harm, why hasn't he fired at me?" Rachel asked.

Again, Griff took his time answering, but judging from the sound of agreement he made, it was probably something he'd already considered. "Maybe he's waiting for a clean shot."

That gave her another jolt of memories. Of her father's shooting. They hadn't seen the gunman that day because she had fired from a heavily treed area behind the police station. But it had indeed been a "clean shot" that went straight into her father's chest. It was a miracle he'd survived.

"We can cut through the back of the alley and then get to my truck that's parked up the street," Griff whispered. "That way you're not out in the open."

"My car is right there," she pointed out. "Only about ten feet away. And the doors are already unlocked."

"If this man wants you dead, he could shoot you before you get inside."

That caused her breath to stop for a moment. Griff normally sugarcoated things for her, but apparently those days were over. Maybe he truly understood that their friendship—and anything else they felt for each other—was over, too.

"There's a deputy," Griff said.

Rachel immediately looked out and spotted a man on foot coming up Main Street. He had his gun drawn and was ducking in and out of doorways of the various shops. He was still three buildings away when the guy who'd been watching them turned and started running out the back of the alley. He quickly disappeared from sight.

"He's getting away," she blurted out.

"The sheriff might have had time to get someone back there." Griff didn't sound very hopeful about that, though. "Come on."

He took hold of her arm to start them moving, and she saw his truck. It was indeed at the back of the alley. But they had barely made it a step before a deafening noise blasted through the air. Not lightning or thunder from the storm. The impact slammed Griff and her into the side of the building.

And that's when Rachel saw that her car had exploded into a giant ball of fire.

Chapter Two

Griff didn't bother to curse himself for not being able to prevent this from happening. No time for cursing and regrets.

He had to get Rachel out of there. And it didn't matter if she no longer trusted him—that explosion should be plenty enough proof to her that someone wanted her dead.

"This way." Griff hooked his arm around her waist to get her moving.

He didn't take her out onto the sidewalk, though. It was too risky for them to go there, because the person who'd just blown up her car could be waiting for them to do just that. Nor did he want to stay put in case there was a second explosion.

The rain started to pelt them, and the lightning suddenly seemed way too close. It definitely wasn't a good time to be outside, especially since there were metal gas pipes leading into the buildings.

"Was that really a bomb?" Rachel asked. Her voice

was as shaky as the rest of her, and she seemed to be talking more to herself than to him.

Griff wasn't sure exactly what it had been. Definitely some kind of explosive device, and that meant someone—probably the guy from the alley—had put it on Rachel's car. He could have done that after she'd parked and gone to the pharmacy, but if so, it was a huge risk. Because someone could have spotted him.

Of course, the idiot could have planted it hours ago and waited until now to detonate it. Even if it didn't kill Rachel and him, it created enough of a diversion for the goon to get away.

Griff kept them moving. Not too fast, though. He needed to try to listen, to make sure someone wasn't coming up behind them.

Or in front of them.

Because it was entirely possible the bomber had a partner somewhere in the maze of alleys. One who could be waiting to ambush them.

"Stay close to me," Griff warned her. "We'll go to my truck."

Rachel immediately started shaking her head. "What if he planted a bomb on it, too?"

"It wasn't out of my sight long enough while I've been here."

Which wasn't long at all. As soon as he'd gotten word that Rachel was in Silver Creek, Griff had come to find her.

Normally, it would have been a forty-five-minute drive from McCall Canyon, but he'd shaved off the minutes to make it in just half an hour. And he was damn lucky he had, too. Because if he hadn't gotten to Rachel in time, she would have tried to get into her car and would have been blown to smithereens.

A thought that felt like a knife to his heart.

Rachel and he weren't a couple. Never had been, really. But Griff wouldn't have forgiven himself if he hadn't been able to save her. And her father wouldn't have forgiven him, either.

"Keep watch behind us," Griff told Rachel, repeating the order he'd given her earlier, and he passed her his phone. "Text the sheriff, Grayson Ryland. That's the last number I called. And tell him where we're going."

He could feel her doing that, hopefully managing to do so while he kept her moving. However, Griff stopped as soon as he made it to the end of the alley. He peered around the corner of the building, but it was too dark to see much of anything. Hearing was a problem, too, thanks to the rain and thunder. He did hear a dinging sound, and figured that meant Rachel had gotten an answer to the text.

"The sheriff says he and his deputy are in pursuit of the guy who was in the alley," she relayed.

Good. Griff didn't want him getting away. If they

caught him, they might finally have answers as to who was trying to kill the McCalls.

And why.

Griff and Rachel's brothers had been investigating that for nearly a month now and had come up empty. Even if Sheriff Ryland and his deputies didn't manage to nab this bomber, maybe they'd be able to get some DNA off the cigarette that the guy had almost certainly ditched somewhere in the alley. Of course, the storm wasn't going to help with that, which meant time was critical right now.

Thanks to another bolt of lightning, Griff was able to get a glimpse of the darker spaces in the alley. He didn't see anyone lurking there, so he stepped out to get a better look.

Not good.

Because all he managed to see was a gun. And that glimpse happened at the exact same moment that a bullet slammed into the brick wall right next to where Griff was standing.

Rachel gave a sharp gasp and grabbed hold of his shoulder, pulling him back just as another shot came at Griff. An inch closer and he would have been a dead man.

Griff cursed and pushed Rachel even deeper into the alley, putting his own body in front of hers. It was far from ideal, mainly because the smoke from the explosion was spilling into the alley and making its way toward them.

Hell.

First an explosion, then lightning. Now a gunshot. This was not the quick in-and-out that Griff had planned for Rachel.

"Did you see the shooter?" she asked. She was shaking even harder now.

"No. But he's to our left." In the opposite direction from Griff's truck. Still, the guy was in the catbird seat right now because he could be hiding behind heaven knew what, just waiting for them to step out so he could shoot them.

Maybe this was the same guy who'd been in the alley across the street. If he knew the layout of the buildings, he could have possibly made his way here. But it was just as likely there were at least two of them.

That didn't help settle Griff's raw nerves.

His phone buzzed, and since Rachel was still holding it, he motioned for her to answer. She did, and even though she didn't put it on speaker, she held the phone close enough for him to hear.

"Did you fire that shot?" Sheriff Ryland asked.

"No. The shooter's somewhere in the alley. I'm taking Rachel back to Main Street."

Shock flashed through her eyes, and Griff could tell from her tensed muscles that she didn't think that was a good idea. He didn't believe it was an especially good one, either, but staying put was too dangerous. If there were indeed two attackers, then they could try to trap Rachel and him in the alley.

"Hold tight for a few more minutes if you can," Sheriff Ryland said. "I'll try to make sure the street is clear."

It was a generous offer, one that Griff accepted, but he knew it was going to be tough for the sheriff to manage. The smoke would be cutting his visibility, too, and they weren't out of the woods yet. There was still the possibility of a second explosion.

Griff moved Rachel to the center of the alley. "Stand with your back to mine and face Main Street," he instructed. That way, he would be in a position to shoot the attacker who'd fired those shots at him.

He took out his reserve weapon from a slide holster in his jeans and handed it to her. Griff prayed she wouldn't need it, but at least if she did, Rachel could shoot. He knew that because he'd been the one to teach her.

That reminder brought back some unwanted thoughts. Rachel's and his lives had been intertwined since he was twelve years old. That's when Griff had moved to McCall Canyon and started doing odd jobs for her father at the McCall Ranch. That meant they had twenty-four years of memories. Some had been bad, really bad, but this would be at the top of the heap.

She took his gun, automatically positioning it the way he'd taught her. Griff hated that he had to put her in this position. Hated that she was in this kind of danger. Later, when they made it out of this, he would need to do something to fix it, to make sure it never happened again.

Of course, Rachel might not let him fix anything. She might try to go on the run again.

"Who's doing this?" she whispered.

"I don't know." Griff wished he did. "But if you've got any ideas, I'm all ears." He expected her to say no.

She didn't.

"Marlon Stowe," she said.

The name meant nothing to Griff, but judging from the way she shuddered, it meant plenty to Rachel.

"Who the hell is he?" Griff demanded.

He wanted to hear every word she said, but he also didn't want anything they were saying to cause him to lose focus. He had to keep watch, and listen, for that shooter.

Rachel shook her head. "It's just some guy who works at the inn where I'm staying. The first week I was there, I saw him and his girlfriend get into a serious argument. I intervened when I thought he was about to hit her, and after the girlfriend and I talked, she broke things off with Marlon and moved out of town. Marlon blames me for that."

Griff was slammed with emotions. Anger that some clown wouldn't leave Rachel alone.

"It's probably not him, though." Rachel gave her head another shake. "I don't think he was mad enough, or crazy enough, to want to kill me."

Griff would soon find out if that was true. Once he had Rachel safe, he would make it a top priority to find out everything he could about this guy. Rachel had been through entirely too much to have to deal with a hothead.

"It's more likely that this is connected to my father and those new threats," Rachel added a moment later.

Griff didn't voice his agreement. Didn't ask her to elaborate, either. That's because he knew what she meant. This could go back to her father's mistress. Or maybe to someone else Warren had ticked off when he'd carried on a three-decades-long affair.

The rain started coming down harder, and Griff felt Rachel shiver. He didn't think it was solely from fear this time. It was May, which meant the temps were already high, but the rain was cold, and their clothes were past the damp stage. The water was starting to stream down their bodies.

His phone dinged again with another text message. "The sheriff says he doesn't see a shooter anywhere near your truck. His deputy is still pursuing the bomber on foot."

Good. Maybe that meant the bomber wouldn't double back. But even if he was trying to do that, it was too dangerous for them to wait around and find out. If the guy had managed to plant one explosive, he could have others on him.

"Let's go," Griff told her.

She nodded, shoved his phone in her pocket and got moving. While they made their way back to the front of the alley, Griff tried to keep watch all around them, and Rachel was doing the same. He prayed it would be enough.

"Stay down," he muttered, when they reached Main Street.

There wasn't much left of her car, but still plenty of flames and smoke. Both could conceal a shooter, but could hopefully give Rachel and him some cover, too.

As he'd done at the back end of the alley, Griff leaned out from the building and looked around. There were plenty of places a shooter could hide. Too many. And Griff didn't see either the sheriff or a deputy. Still, he couldn't wait any longer.

"Keep low and watch where you're stepping," Griff warned her.

In addition to the limited visibility from the smoke, there were bits of car parts, metal and glass all over the sidewalk. He didn't want Rachel getting tripped up once they started to move.

Griff took out his truck keys, said a quick prayer and stayed in front of Rachel when they stepped out from cover. He didn't have to tell her to move fast because she did it automatically. She also started to cough.

The smoke quickly began to burn his eyes, so Griff picked up the pace as much as he could. He also continued to keep watch. Especially behind them. He didn't want that shooter coming out of the alley and gunning them down.

It seemed to take way too long to get to his truck, and the moment he reached it, he unlocked the driver's-side door and threw it open. He was about to push Rachel inside when he heard a sound. Not on the street.

But from above.

Griff glanced up just in time to spot the man on the roof of the one-story building. Even though he didn't have a good view of the guy's face, he had no trouble seeing his gun. A gun the man fired.

The bullet ripped through the rear window on his truck and exited the windshield. The only reason it missed Rachel was because she moved a split second before the guy pulled the trigger. She dived across the seat, and in the same motion caught Griff's arm to pull him in, as well.

He shook off her grip, turned and took aim, firing two shots at the man on the roof.

That sent the guy ducking for cover, and Griff took advantage of that. While he would have liked to go after this moron and arrest him, he couldn't put Rachel at risk like that. He had to get her out of here. And not just off Main Street and out of the line of sight of this shooter. He needed to get her away from Silver Creek and whatever the heck was going on here. He had to take her to McCall Canyon so they could regroup and catch these SOBs.

Griff jumped behind the wheel, got the engine started and hit the accelerator.

"Get down!" he warned Rachel.

She did.

Just as bullets slammed into the back window.

Chapter Three

Griff and she had managed to get away from a killer.

She kept reminding herself of that. Kept reminding herself, too, that they were alive. But it might be a long time before that all sank in. Especially since the would-be killer had managed to escape. He was still out there. Maybe regrouping. Perhaps planning another attack. And maybe next time, Griff and she wouldn't be so lucky.

With that terrifying possibility going through her mind, Rachel looked out at the McCall Canyon sheriff's office when Griff pulled to a stop in front of it. She took a deep breath, trying to steel herself.

It didn't work.

Of course, there wasn't much that would help steady her right now. She was going to have to face her family, and there probably wasn't enough steel in her backbone to get her through that. Because she was already close to the breaking point.

If Griff hadn't pulled her into that alley when

he did, she would have died in the car explosion. Ditto for him getting her to his truck so they could get away. While she was very glad to be alive, she couldn't forget that in those blink-of-an-eye moments, the outcome could have been a whole lot different. Griff and she could both be dead.

"Thank you," she told him.

He'd already reached to open the door of his truck, but he stopped and looked at her as if she'd lost her mind. That's when she realized he'd misinterpreted what she'd said.

"I'm not thanking you for bringing me here," Rachel corrected. "But for saving my life."

Griff just sat there, perhaps waiting for something else. Maybe for her to blast him for finding her when she'd made it so clear that she hadn't wanted to be found. She hadn't wanted him in her life, either. However, that was an argument that could wait. For now, she had two other items on the agenda.

Her brothers.

Both Court and Egan were right there in the squad room when Griff and she went in. Anyone who saw her brothers together like this had no doubt they were related. They had the same dark brown hair and intense gray eyes. Rachel had obviously gotten their mother's genes, since her hair was blond and her eyes blue. Still, there was enough family resemblance for people to tell she was a McCall, too.

Thankfully, there were no other lawmen around, not even a dispatcher. And she was especially thankful that her father wasn't here. Since this probably wasn't going to be a pleasant conversation, Rachel preferred that as few people as possible were present.

Griff's phone dinged with a text message—something that had been happening during most of the drive from Silver Creek. He'd had Rachel read those to him so he could focus on the drive, but he didn't make that offer now. He stepped to the side, probably not only to read the text but to give her some time with Egan and Court.

As Griff had done in the truck, her brothers just stared at her for a moment. They looked her over from head to toe, their gazes lingering on the jacket she was wearing.

It was Griff's.

He'd given it to her in the truck when she'd started shaking. Not just because she was wet from the rain, but because the adrenaline had still been slamming into her. She'd gladly accepted the jacket. And had tried not to notice that it carried Griff's scent.

Rachel failed at that, too. She noticed.

Court was the first to budge. He cursed—the profanity definitely meant for her—and then he pulled her into his arms. "Leaving town like that was a really stupid thing to do," he whispered to her, while he brushed a kiss on her cheek.

"I didn't have a choice," she whispered back.

Court pulled away, studied her eyes, then he nodded. Perhaps that meant he understood that what their father had done had shaken her so badly that she'd needed to put some distance between them. What Court probably didn't know was that the deepest cut had come from Griff.

Again, though, that was an argument with Griff she'd need to postpone, because she had to face Egan. Unlike Court, he didn't come to her. Her other brother stood there, giving her one of his infamous glares that no doubt worked on criminals. Not kid sisters, though. Rachel went to him and hugged him. It was like hugging a statue, because his muscles were rock hard. But then she felt him relax.

"I was worried about you," he said against her ear. "Don't you *ever* make me worry about you like that again."

No need for her to tell him that she'd been concerned, too. Not just with leaving McCall Canyon, but with everything that had gone on tonight. Concerned and scared. All their lives had changed on a dime when their father had been shot, and the changes apparently weren't over yet. Griff had said there were new threats, and with the attack, it could mean the person who'd made those threats wasn't finished with her family.

Or not.

This might not be connected at all, which made it all the more frustrating. Someone wanted her dead, and she not only didn't know who, Rachel didn't know why.

"Griff said you weren't hurt," Egan added. "Is it true?"

"I'm okay," she settled for saying.

He let the hug linger a few more seconds before he moved back and looked at Griff. "Tell me how we catch the SOB who tried to kill Rachel."

On the drive over, Griff had filled Egan in on the basics while on speakerphone. Well, he'd done that after they'd been sure the shooter wasn't following them. He had also had several conversations with Sheriff Ryland.

What Griff hadn't done was talked to Rachel.

Like Egan, he was clearly still fuming that she'd left town and then had gotten herself into a dangerous situation. She hadn't purposely run toward the danger. She'd been running to get away from Griff and her father. Now, here she was—right back with them. Or at least she soon would be with both of them because she was certain that either Egan or Court had already called their father.

Griff quit reading the text on his phone and shifted his attention to Egan. "Sheriff Ryland is getting us footage from a security camera outside a bank that was just up the street from where Rachel had her car parked. We might be able to see who planted the explosive device."

Rachel wasn't holding out hope. If the guy was bold enough to do something like that on Main Street, then he was probably aware of the position of the camera. Still, they might get lucky. If not, maybe someone had even seen the person and could give them a description.

Egan hooked his arm around her and got her moving to his office, which was at the back of the squad room. Once he had her there, he practically sat her in the chair next to his desk, then got her a bottle of water from his fridge.

She'd been in this office many times—when it'd been her father's, and then for the past four years since it was Egan's. It hadn't changed in, well, forever. Same desk. Same filing cabinet. Same fridge.

The picture was there on the wall, of course. A photo of Egan, Court, her and their late brother, Warren Jr.— or W.J. as folks had called him. W.J. had been dead for nearly a decade now. Shot and killed in the line of duty when he'd been a deputy sheriff on call at a domestic dispute that had turned deadly.

The pain and grief from losing him felt as fresh as if she'd just lost him hours ago instead of all those years. That was the picture she had in her head. Her brother dead. His life cut much too short because he'd been wearing a badge and trying to do the right thing.

And that was the reason Rachel had sworn she would never fall for a cop.

That included a Texas Ranger like Griff.

"Tell me about this dirtbag who's riled at you," Egan insisted.

That was his big-brother tone, and it caused her to sigh. Egan had always been protective of her, which was why he often shot Griff scowling looks. Like now. Neither their father nor Egan had ever thought Griff was the right man for her. And he wasn't. He'd proved that last month.

"His name is Marlon Stowe," Rachel answered, after she had a long sip of the water. "His folks own the inn where I was staying, and he works part-time in the office there. He believes I'm responsible for his girlfriend leaving him. I suppose I am," she added.

"I've already requested a background check on him," Griff explained. "I'm waiting on a call about him now." He took out his phone and showed her the photo on the screen. "That's the guy, right?"

She nodded. It was Marlon's DMV photo that Griff had apparently gotten in that text. "His hair's a little lighter in this picture than it was the last time I saw him." Marlon definitely didn't look like a cowboy. He had the clean and polished appearance of a businessman. One with a tense edge to him.

"Checking out Marlon is a good start," Rachel continued. "He gives me the creeps, but he hasn't been around the inn for the last week or so. Plus, he's never been...actually physically aggressive. He just made it very clear that he was furious with me because I convinced his girlfriend to leave him." She paused. "You're sure our half brother or our father's mistress isn't behind this?"

Griff quickly shook his head. "Your half brother is a cop. And no, there's no indication whatsoever that he's dirty. His name is Raleigh Lawton, by the way. He's a county sheriff."

She knew that. Rachel hadn't been able to resist looking him up online. "We're certain Raleigh is really Warren's son?"

"Warren says he is," Griff confirmed. "Raleigh refused to have a DNA test. He wants nothing to do with Warren, your brothers or you."

Rachel didn't fault him for that, since she felt the same way about Warren. "How about his mother then?"

Her name was Alma Lawton. Rachel knew plenty about her, too, but it wasn't *plenty enough* to understand why her father had carried on an affair with the woman and had a child with her.

"I've already called Alma," Court said. "She'll be in first thing in the morning for questioning."

Rachel was betting the woman wouldn't care much for that, and it almost certainly wasn't the first time her brothers or Griff had brought the woman in. No.

Because Alma was once a person of interest in her father's shooting and could have been connected to the actual shooter, Whitney. After all, Alma had been his mistress for years, and it was possible she'd just gotten tired of waiting for Warren to leave his family for her.

But that wasn't motive for Alma to go after one of Warren's kids.

Was it?

Maybe if the woman wanted to punish Warren, she might believe that was the way to do it. But there were a lot of "ifs" in that theory. It was possible that Alma was the one who'd ended the longtime affair, and if so, that would mean she didn't have a motive for what was going on.

"We haven't told Mom about the attack," Court went on. "We thought that was best, considering."

Yes, considering that their mother was in a mental hospital. That was something else she could thank her father for doing. Hearing the news of her husband's affair and his other life had sent Helen over the edge.

"I won't say anything when I talk to her," Rachel assured them. Which would be soon. Rachel had been calling her every day for the past month, and she wouldn't miss the call tomorrow, either.

"You haven't asked about Dad," Egan said. He didn't wait for her to respond. "He got out of the hospital about two weeks ago, and he's upset that you ran off before he had a chance to explain."

Rachel could practically feel her blood pressure soaring. "Well, you can tell him I'm upset that he couldn't be faithful to his wife."

She didn't bother to take the venom out of her voice but hated that she'd aimed it at Egan. Court was more of the forgiving sort and had probably worked out a way to make amends with Warren, but Egan was likely just as bitter about this as she was. The difference was that he hadn't left.

Egan grunted in agreement and tipped his head to Griff, sending another scowl his way. "Griff told us what happened between you two the night Dad was shot. That you landed in bed for comfort sex."

Rachel snapped toward Griff so fast that her neck popped. She was certain *she* was scowling at him now.

"I thought they needed to hear what'd happened," Griff said, his mouth tight. "I wanted them to know that you might have left because of me and not Warren."

"I left because of both of you," she snapped. And intended to say a whole lot more to Griff—in private.

Mercy. He had no right to tell her family about that.

"I'm guessing it's over between Griff and you?" Egan asked.

"Yes." Rachel snapped that response, too.

And she scowled at Egan when he gave her that big-brother look again. Egan didn't have to come out and say it, but she felt a mental lecture coming on. One where he would say something about hoping she'd remembered to practice safe sex. She had.

Or rather, Griff had.

They'd used a condom, but with the way her life had been going, she'd taken a pregnancy test two weeks later just in case. It'd been negative. So at least her mistake of sleeping with Griff hadn't resulted in a pregnancy.

The mental lecture was still going on between Egan and her when the front door opened. Griff, Court and Egan all reacted by drawing their guns. But they all soon holstered them again, Court and Griff making grumbling sounds. Rachel knew the reason for the grumbles.

Their visitor was the district attorney, Brad Gandy.

It was an understatement that Brad and Griff didn't get along. She was the main reason for that. Brad had always had a thing for her. And Court had been on Griff's side. In fact, Court was the only McCall who'd ever wanted to see Griff and her together. Of course, that probably didn't apply now that Court knew Griff had slept with her while keeping Warren's dirty little secret.

Brad made a beeline to Egan's office, volleying

glances at all of them when he stepped inside. His eyes narrowed a bit when his attention landed on Griff. Griff's only reaction was to scowl even harder than he already was.

The two men were definitely a huge contrast. Brad, in his pricey gray suit, looked as if he'd just stepped out of the courtroom. Griff was pure cowboy in his jeans and Stetson.

"Rachel," Brad said on a rise of breath when he'd finished with his glances. "I heard about someone trying to kill you. God, I'm so sorry." He went straight to her and pulled her into his arms.

She tried not to go stiff. After all, Brad and she had once dated in college, and he'd hugged and kissed her back then. However, it didn't feel right for that little display of affection to happen in front of her brothers. Or Griff.

Especially Griff.

Rachel silently cursed him. And the blasted attraction. She wished she could make herself immune to him.

Brad eased back, making eye contact with her. Except it wasn't just mere contact. He was looking at her as if examining her, to make sure she was all right. She wasn't, but Rachel tried to appear a lot stronger than she felt as she stepped out of his grip.

"How'd you know about the attack?" she asked, and she prayed it wasn't on the news. Rachel didn't want her mother to find out that way—or any other way, for that matter.

Brad flinched a little. Maybe because her tone had been so brusque. Or maybe because she hadn't greeted him with the same enthusiastic hug he'd given her. "I'm friends with the DA in Silver Creek."

She glanced at Griff, and before she could voice her concern about that, he took out his phone once more. "I'll make sure no one at the hospital mentions it to your mother." He stepped outside the office to make the call.

Rachel made a mental note to thank him for that, too. Another mental note to make arrangements to put some distance between Griff and her. She needed to think, and right now, her head wasn't cooperating. She was dizzy and exhausted, and being around Griff had a way of making her not think straight. The blasted attraction kept getting in the way.

"Are you really okay?" Court asked her.

That's when Rachel realized she was massaging her right temple. "I'm not about to have a seizure. And I've been taking my meds."

Of course, that didn't mean a seizure wouldn't happen, but if it did, there was nothing she could do to stop it now.

"Please tell me you know who tried to murder Rachel," Brad said to Egan.

Egan lifted his shoulder. "Sorry, my ESP isn't

working so great tonight. But I've got a lead, and I'll question Alma Lawton."

"Alma!" Brad spat out the name like he would profanity. Maybe some of his tone was due to Egan's smart-mouthed remark. "Yes, definitely talk to her. She hates every one of you. What kind of lead do you have?" he pressed.

Egan hesitated, as if debating if he would tell him. Brad and he were on the same side of the law, but Rachel figured sometimes it didn't feel that way. They'd butted heads on several cases over the years. However, Rachel thought the underlying current was because Egan didn't want her to be with Brad any more than he wanted her to be with Griff.

At the moment, she felt the same way—despite the simmering heat between Griff and her. There was heat, too, when it came to Brad, but it was all one-sided.

"Marlon Stowe," Egan finally answered. "He's a guy who might blame Rachel for his girlfriend leaving him. Did the Silver Creek district attorney happen to mention him to you?"

Judging from the way Brad's mouth tightened, that would be a no. "When are you bringing him in for questioning?"

Egan shrugged. "When I've got probable cause, and right now—"

"You've got it," Griff interrupted, stepping back

into the room. He looked at Egan and then tipped his head to the laptop on the desk. "First things first. Sheriff Ryland just emailed you the surveillance footage from the bank camera."

That sent both Court and Egan to the computer. Rachel would have joined them, but it was obvious Griff had something else to say.

"Marlon's ex-girlfriend from a year ago took out a restraining order against him because he was stalking her," Griff continued. "Sheriff Ryland said Marlon also hit her, but she wouldn't press charges against him. There are rumors that he hit his last girlfriend, Taryn Harrison, too. That's the woman you saw with Marlon while you were staying at the inn."

Yes, and Marlon blamed her for the breakup. Rachel felt the chill slide through her. Here, she'd left McCall Canyon to escape, and instead she'd crossed paths with a bully. One who might be unhinged if he was indeed into stalking.

Brad turned toward her. "See? This is why you should have never left," he snapped. "Did that man touch you?"

"No. He just said I should mind my own business." She stopped, thought of something else. "But the next time we crossed paths, he seemed to know who I was. I mean, I was using an alias. I'd told everyone there at the inn that my name was Margaret O'Malley."

"Mom's middle and maiden names," Court supplied, looking up from the laptop. Egan kept his attention planted firmly on the screen.

She nodded. "I lied and told them I didn't have any ID because my wallet had been stolen. I used cash to pay for the room."

"Cash that you withdrew from your bank account right before you left town," Brad said.

So obviously he'd checked on that. That wasn't a surprise, not really. They'd probably all been looking for her. It was ironic that Griff had been the one to find her.

"What made you think Marlon knew who you were?" Griff asked.

She almost dismissed it, but that would mean dismissing the knot in her stomach. After what'd happened, it was best if she listened to it.

"When I was paying for my room last week, Marlon was in the office, and he wrote the receipt," she explained. "He started writing my name with an *R*, then he quickly scratched it out and wrote 'Margaret' instead. I think he'd been about to put down 'Rachel.'"

Brad made a sound to indicate he was giving that some thought. "Maybe he saw you on the news. After Warren's shooting," he clarified.

It was possible, but Griff didn't look as if he was buying it, either. Good. She wanted him and her brothers to dig into Marlon's activities and see if there was something to find.

"Hell," Egan said. "There's someone on the footage."

Brad hurried behind the desk to have a look, but Griff stayed right next to her. Egan turned the screen so they could see, and it didn't take long for her to realize they were looking at the man who'd been in the alley.

A man she instantly recognized.

Oh, God.

Chapter Four

What the hell was Warren doing on the Silver Creek surveillance video?

That was the question Griff was very anxious to ask the man. Apparently, he wasn't the only one who had an urgent need to know, because Rachel whipped out her phone and pressed in her father's number. Since Griff had been about to do the same thing, he just waited for Warren to answer.

But he didn't.

After a few rings, the call went to voice mail. "Call me now," was all that Rachel snapped into the phone when she left her father a message.

Since Warren was worried about Rachel and had spent the past month trying to find her, he would no doubt do just that. Well, he would unless he'd done something stupid.

"It appears you've got a new person of interest," Brad said, his mouth tight and his eyes narrowed as he stared at the screen.

Griff didn't like that Brad had jumped to the worst-case scenario. Of course, he'd never been a fan of Warren, because they, too, had clashed when Warren had been sheriff.

"It doesn't make sense," Griff said to Rachel. "Warren wouldn't hurt you. He wouldn't hurt any of his kids."

"Not unless he was finished with me," Rachel quickly pointed out. But even she had to wave that off. "No. He wouldn't hurt me. Not intentionally, anyway." She pointed to the screen. "So why is he there?"

Griff had a theory, and this was going to be a good news/bad news kind of deal. "Maybe Warren found out where you were and went to check on you." That was the good news. "And maybe while Warren was watching you, he could have gotten caught up in the attack."

After everything she'd been through tonight, Griff hated to point that out to her, but Rachel was smart and would have soon come to the same conclusion. Plus, that was still better than thinking Warren could have had any part in that explosion or the shots being fired.

"I'll call the Silver Creek sheriff," Egan volunteered, taking out his phone, as well.

"And it might be jumping the gun, but I'll see if I can have Dad's cell phone traced," Court added. He stepped away as if to start doing just that, but then volleyed glances at Brad, Griff and his sister before his attention settled on Griff. "Why don't you go ahead and get Rachel out of here so she can get some rest?"

Since Rachel was no doubt on the verge of an adrenaline crash, that was a good idea, but judging from the way her forehead bunched up, it was going to be hard for Griff to sell her on doing that. He definitely didn't want to use her epilepsy to get her to leave. Over the years, he'd learned that she didn't want any special considerations because of it. Still, the stress might trigger a seizure. He'd been with her once when that'd happened. They'd been teenagers then, but he'd never forgotten it.

"I can take Rachel to my place," Brad suggested. "I've got a great security system, and it's not somewhere that the gunman would expect her to go."

Griff wanted to nix that suggestion right off, but had to admit that was because he didn't like Brad. He didn't want Rachel under Brad's roof at any time, but especially not when she was so vulnerable.

Of course, that might be his own guilty conscience at work. Rachel had certainly been vulnerable after learning of her father's affair, and that hadn't stopped Griff from sleeping with her.

Apparently, Rachel had her own concerns about Brad, however, because she shook her head. "Thanks, but your place is over a half hour's drive from here.

I don't want to be that far from the sheriff's office in case they catch the shooter. I want to be here if they get a chance to question him."

Griff figured there was no way to stop her from observing the interview. No way to stop him, either, since this idiot had nearly killed Rachel and him. But first they had to catch the guy, and he was most likely long gone by now.

"If you don't want to ride all the way out to the ranch," Griff suggested to her, "my house is closer."

She looked at him, and he saw the concern she had about that. Rightfully so. The last time she'd been at his house, they'd landed in bed. No way would that happen again. Not now, maybe not ever.

"The Silver Creek cops haven't seen Dad," Egan relayed when he got off the phone. "But they'll look for him while they continue their search for the shooter."

Maybe they'd get lucky and find both. Griff just didn't want the cops to find Warren and the gunman together. Because if that happened, it meant Warren was either a hostage or had been involved in some way. That involvement might not necessarily be of his own doing, though.

"There's nothing else you can do here," Court chimed in, glancing at Rachel. "Griff could drive you to the ranch or his place, and I could follow to make sure you get there all right."

In other words, Court would go to make sure they weren't attacked along the way. It was a possibility, but since the other attack had happened on Main Street in Silver Creek, the ranch was probably safer than keeping her here. The ranch had a security gate, so someone couldn't just come driving through. Of course, there were fences that could be scaled, which meant Griff would need to alert the hands to keep an eye out for anyone suspicious.

Rachel huffed and then finally nodded. "The ranch. It'll give me a chance to catch up on some paperwork that I'm sure has been piling up since I've been gone."

It had been, because Griff had heard Warren, Court and Egan complaining about it. Normally, Warren and his sons handled the livestock supply, but Rachel managed the ranch's finances and day-to-day operation. The McCall Ranch was big so it was a full-time job. With Warren recovering from the shooting and Rachel's mom in the hospital, the business side of things had been neglected during Rachel's absence, and it was costing the McCalls business.

"Does this mean you're moving back?" Court asked.

"No." Rachel didn't hesitate, either. "But I'll try to organize the paperwork so that whoever Dad hires to take my place will have an easier transition." She paused. "I don't want the ranch to lose business, for Egan's and your sakes. It's your home."

Court went to her, brushed a kiss on her forehead. "It's your home, too. And you don't have to stay under Dad's roof. You can do what I did and build a place of your own on the ranch grounds."

She gave no indication whatsoever that she would consider that, but she did give her brother's arm a gentle squeeze. Maybe Court would be able to help mend the fences between Warren and Rachel. Of course, there was a lot of mending to be done, and now that had to include a good explanation of why Warren had been in Silver Creek tonight.

"Rachel, I can drive you out to the ranch," Brad volunteered. "That way, Griff could stay here and work the investigation. I'm sure he has plenty to do."

Griff did have plenty, but he could do it at the ranch. He also didn't like the way Brad was pushing this.

"We don't need Griff here," Court argued. Griff really needed to buy Court a drink for that. "And I'd rather Rachel be with a lawman. No offense, but if the shooter comes back, a Texas Ranger would be better able to protect her than a DA."

Brad's mouth went tight again, and he looked at Rachel, no doubt hoping that she would choose him over Griff for protective custody.

Rachel glanced at both of them and took a deep

breath before she answered. "I'll go with Griff. But I'll be at the ranch just for tonight. I'll make other arrangements tomorrow."

It didn't sound as if she wanted Griff in on those arrangements, but there was no way Egan and Court would just let their kid sister go someplace that wasn't safe. Well, as safe as they could make it, anyway.

"We can use the cruisers out front," Court suggested, and he turned to Griff. "I can have someone bring your truck to you."

Griff thanked him, and after Rachel said a quick goodbye to Egan, she followed Court and Griff to the front. Court went out first, glancing around to make sure no one was out there. Once Court had given him the all clear, Griff got Rachel moving as fast as he could. Brad was right behind them, and for a moment Griff thought the man might try to get into the cruiser with them, but he stopped at the passenger door. He kept his attention nailed to Rachel as if he hoped she would change her mind.

She didn't.

Rachel looked everywhere but at Brad as Griff drove away. He spared the DA just a glance, to make sure he stayed put, but Griff was more interested in making sure Court was right behind them and that no one else pulled out to follow them. He didn't see another vehicle other than Court's cruiser and hoped it stayed that way.

"Sorry about this," Griff said. "I know you don't want to be with me—"

"I don't." Then she paused. "But I don't want to die. Nor do I want to tie up Egan and Court to baby-sit me."

She probably had meant that to be a dig, and Griff didn't mind if it was. He didn't want to tie up her brothers, either. He needed them to focus on catching whoever was behind the attack. Griff would help with that, too, but the sheriff's office wasn't his jurisdiction, and he could work the case from his laptop.

"This doesn't mean things are good between us." Rachel tacked that onto her comment.

He nodded. "It won't make sense to you, but I don't want things to be *good* between us. I screwed up, and I don't expect you to ever forgive me for it."

Her expression let him know that she wasn't buying that he was being genuine about that. Well, she should. Because it was true. If it'd been just keeping Warren's secret, then in time she might have relented. But Griff had slept with her, and he didn't see a way past that.

Since their *relationship* was a touchy subject, Griff moved on to something else. Something that could end up being touchy, too, but he was getting a bad feeling in his gut about the DA.

"Is it my imagination or is Brad…clinging more than usual when it comes to you?" Griff asked.

She shot him a look as if that was something she might not want to discuss with him before she sighed. "He's clingy," she confirmed. "Before things fell apart at home, Brad had been pressuring me to go out with him again. And you should know that my father was encouraging it."

That didn't surprise Griff, but it still stung. It was also a reminder that as much as he loved Warren, Warren had never felt Griff was worthy of Rachel. And he wasn't. But it bothered Griff that Warren thought Brad was the right man for his daughter. Brad wasn't anywhere near good enough for her, but then Griff admitted that he was biased about that.

"I think Dad was starting to believe I'd become an old maid," she added in a grumble.

Nowhere close to that. Rachel was only thirty-one. Since Griff was five years older, that'd been another reason Warren had wanted him to keep his distance from Rachel. It had been a big deal when she was just sixteen, but no longer seemed an obstacle. However, there were other obstacles now, including the fact that Rachel might never trust him again.

Griff continued to look around. So did Rachel, and because she was so quiet he heard the rhythm of her breathing change. For one heart-stopping moment, he thought it was because she'd seen someone lying

in wait for them, but he soon figured out it was because the ranch had come into view.

He hated that this place was no longer a sanctu-
ary for her. No longer a home. And he wondered if
it ever would be again. Her mother would be getting
out of the mental hospital soon, and it was entirely
possible that Helen would file for a divorce. No one
would fault her if she did. But that meant one of Rachel's parents would almost certainly move.

Griff turned onto the ranch road and immediately
spotted several hands near the gate. They opened it
for him, and he drove through. As planned, Court
turned around and headed back toward town. Griff
kept watch in the rearview mirror to make sure the
hands closed the gate behind them. They did.

Rachel eyed the main house and then Court's
place, which was just up the road. "Is Rayna living
there now?" she asked.

Rayna Travers was Court's girlfriend and likely
soon to be his fiancée. "No. Not yet. She's still living
at her place." A small horse ranch not far from there.

Rachel's eyes widened. "She's not alone, is she?
Because the shooter could go there."

He quickly shook his head. "She's at a horse show
in Dallas. I'm sure Court has someone watching out
for her."

In fact, there was no doubt in Griff's mind about

that. Court was clearly in love with Rayna and would take plenty of precautions to make sure she was safe. Ditto for taking those precautions for his sister. Both Court and Egan would work this case to make sure the danger ended fast. Griff just hoped it was fast enough that there wouldn't be another attack.

"So far, Rayna hasn't been included in the new threats we've been getting," Griff added.

"*We?* You've been getting them, too?"

He nodded. "Court, Egan and your dad, as well. And your mom. Obviously, we haven't let her know about that, and yes, we've alerted the hospital. Egan hired a private guard to watch her."

The guard wasn't only because of the new threats, though. It was because a month earlier someone had kidnapped the woman, and Egan and Court wanted to make sure that didn't happen again.

A heavy sigh left Rachel's mouth. "How bad are the threats?"

Bad. In fact, they still twisted away at him. And while he would have liked to have sheltered Rachel from knowing the exact words, he wouldn't keep this from her. He'd learned his lesson about doing that. Besides, if he sugarcoated it, she might not take it as seriously as she should.

"The person who sent them wants Warren to suffer," Griff answered. "He or she says Warren will watch his children die one by one until he has nothing left but misery in his life."

Rachel shuddered and turned away from him. "Please tell me you have a suspect."

"Too many of them," he admitted. "Along with Alma Lawton, who could be connected to Whitney, there are plenty of criminals who'd like to get back at Warren for arresting them. We're making our way through the case files now."

But the investigation was moving at a snail's pace since they were basically having to use the looking-for-a-needle-in-a-haystack approach. Because it might not be an actual convicted criminal who was doing this, but rather someone connected to a person who Warren had managed to convict. Warren had made more enemies than friends during his long reign as the sheriff of McCall Canyon. He'd made an ample share of enemies in his business dealings, too. So, yeah, definitely slow going.

Rachel looked up at the house when Griff pulled to a stop in front of it. The porch lights were on, and Griff spotted one of the hands in a truck parked in the side driveway.

"You know the drill," Griff reminded her. "Move fast."

She did. Rachel got out of the cruiser and hurried up the porch steps, but the door opened before they reached it. Griff automatically went for his gun, but it was only Ruby, the McCalls' longtime cook and housekeeper. The woman was more family than employee, and immediately pulled Rachel into a hug.

"I'm so glad you're home," Ruby whispered to her.

Griff hated to cut the reunion short, but he didn't want Rachel out in the open any longer than necessary. That's why he took both women by the arm and maneuvered them inside.

"Are you all right?" Ruby asked, pushing Rachel's hair from her face. "Egan called and said there'd been some more trouble. I figured we'd already had enough of that."

"We have," Rachel assured her. "And I'm fine."

No, she wasn't. She looked ready to collapse, and Ruby must have noticed.

"Should I do anything special to be certain that she stays safe?" Ruby asked Griff.

"Make sure all the windows and doors are locked and set the security system. I'll call the head ranch hand and see where he has guards posted." Griff took out his phone to do that, but Rachel's cell rang.

She sucked in her breath when she saw the screen, so Griff knew this was important. He went to her and saw the name.

Warren.

Rachel's hand was trembling when she pressed the button to put it on speaker. "Where are you?" she snapped.

"Rachel?" It was Warren all right, but he sounded groggy or something. "Is that you?"

"Of course it's me. You called my phone, remember?"

"What?" Warren mumbled something else that Griff didn't catch. "Are you all right?"

"No, I'm not," she answered, her tone edged with anger. "Are you in Silver Creek? And did you attack Griff and me tonight?"

Griff expected Warren to jump to deny that last question. He didn't. Instead, Warren groaned. "Someone tried to hurt you," he said, but he slurred his words, making Griff wonder if the man was drunk.

"No, someone tried to *kill* me. Was it you?" Rachel demanded, her voice much louder than before.

"God, Rachel." Warren groaned again. "I'm so sorry. But I just don't know."

Chapter Five

Rachel paced across the living room of the ranch house, each time checking out the huge bay window as she walked past it. There was no sign of Egan or her father yet, but according to Egan's last text, they should be here any minute.

Maybe then she could get answers.

Answers that she certainly hadn't gotten the night before, when her father had called her. He'd sounded disoriented, maybe even drunk, but she'd never witnessed him having more than a beer or two. Certainly not enough alcohol to make him forget where he was. Or if he'd had something to do with the attacks.

She heard Griff's footsteps, but even before she could see him, he grumbled out a warning. Probably because he heard her footsteps, too. "The pacing won't help. They'll get here just as fast if you're sitting."

Yes, but there was no way she could sit with all this restless energy inside her.

Griff came from the direction of the kitchen, carrying two mugs. She could tell from the smell that one was the strong coffee he favored. The other was her usual tea, which he handed to her.

"Ruby fixed it," Griff added, "so it should be good."

Rachel had a sip, nodded. It was exactly the way she liked it, and she made a mental note to thank Ruby the next time the woman came in to check on her. Which would no doubt be very soon. Ruby had been making those checks ever since Griff and she had arrived at the ranch the night before, and the frequency had increased in the past hour, since Egan's text.

"I talked to Court a couple of minutes ago," Griff said. "Your father is more lucid this morning."

"But?" Rachel definitely heard the uncertainty in his voice.

"But he has some memory gaps about last night. In other words, don't expect him to be able to tell us a lot more than we already know."

She shook her head. "He has to tell us more. I need to know why he was in that alley."

Griff made a sound of agreement and sipped his coffee. He didn't sit, but instead joined her at the bay window. At first she thought that was because he was anxious to see Egan and Warren, too, but he gently took hold of her arm and moved her back. Only then did she remember that it probably wasn't safe to stand in plain view like that, because there could be a sniper in the area.

She silently cursed. She hated that she had to be cautioned about that kind of threat in a place where she'd once felt so safe.

"I just assumed if the doctor released Dad from the hospital, it meant his memory had fully returned," Rachel grumbled.

She didn't really expect Griff to have an answer to that, because he'd already told her the details of his conversations with both her brothers. Her father had had an overnight stay because the doctor had wanted to run tests on him to see why he was so disoriented. The tests had been inconclusive, but all the results weren't in yet. She was hoping when they had those results back, they'd have answers to go along with them.

Rachel got up and went to the window again when she heard the sound of an approaching vehicle, and spotted Egan's cruiser as he pulled to a stop in front of the house. She'd thought she had steeled herself enough to see her father. She hadn't. When he got out of the car, he looked frail and old. It seemed as if he'd aged a decade in the past month.

Griff went to the front door and opened it after he disarmed the security system, then he helped Egan get

Warren up the steps. Her father was short of breath by the time he made it inside.

"Rachel." His gaze immediately connected with hers, but he didn't come toward her. Probably because he didn't want to risk her turning away from him.

She nodded a greeting, and because she suddenly felt a little unsteady, sank down onto one of the chairs in the family room. Griff led her father in there, too, and had him sit across from her.

"Nothing yet on the rest of the test results," Egan volunteered. "The doctor wants Dad to take it easy for a day or two."

"I don't want to take it easy," Warren immediately protested. "I want to find the person who tried to kill Griff and Rachel. Because I'm betting that's the same person who did this to me. He must have drugged me. My guess is it was some kind of barbiturate, since I've got memory loss."

Yes, Rachel suspected that, as well, but her father wasn't in any shape to go looking for a would-be killer. But that did lead her to something that had been eating away at her.

"If the shooter got close enough to you, then why just drug you?" she asked her father.

Warren shook his head. "I don't know. If he wanted me dead, he could have killed me then."

He took the words right out of her mouth. Words that chilled her to the bone. Because this monster could be toying with them. Or maybe her father wasn't even the target.

Maybe she was.

And that led her right back to Marlon.

Of course, it could be Alma, too, if she'd wanted to punish Warren by making him witness the death of his daughter. Rachel hoped Egan and Griff didn't give her any hassles about watching the interviews they had scheduled with both of them. Not that she expected either of them to blurt out confessions, but they might say something to give them away.

"What exactly do you remember about what went on last night?" Griff asked Warren.

That caused Rachel to shift her attention back to her father, but after one look at his downcast expression, she doubted he was going to give them much. Still, anything was a start.

He dragged in a long breath before he started. "I went to a bar in San Antonio to meet with Buddy Hoskins. I thought he might know something about who was sending us those threats."

Buddy Hoskins. She knew the name. Buddy was one of her father's criminal informants when he'd still been sheriff. From what Rachel could remember, the man had a drug habit and a long arrest record. Her father had never brought him to the house, but she'd seen him once at the sheriff's office.

"Why would Buddy know anything about the threats?" Griff pressed.

"He didn't say when he texted me to set up the meeting. Buddy just said he'd heard some talk and wanted to pass it along to me. I figured the reason he wanted to tell me in person was so I'd give him some cash."

That didn't surprise her, but considering everything that had gone on, the meeting could have been a setup.

"Buddy texted you," Griff said. "Is that the way he usually gets in touch with you?"

"Sometimes. Usually he calls, though." Warren groaned and scrubbed his hand over his forehead. "You think it was someone else who sent that text, to lure me to that bar?"

"Possibly. Did you actually meet with Buddy?" Griff pressed.

"I don't think so. If I did, I don't recall seeing him. I got to the bar, ordered a beer and the next thing I remember is waking up in the hospital. Everything in between is a blank."

"For now it is," Egan said. "The doctor thought there was a chance you might get those memories back in a day or two."

Rachel sighed before she could stop herself. A day or two might be too late for Griff and her. Heck, for all of them.

Egan checked his watch and then looked at Griff. "Can you hold things down here while I go back to the station? I've got a mountain of paperwork to do before the interviews."

Griff nodded, though he did cast an uneasy glance at Rachel. Maybe because he wasn't certain how she felt about being in the same house with her father. She wasn't certain about how she felt, either, but it wasn't safe for her to leave until she'd made other arrangements. Something she needed to get started on, since it was obvious she wasn't going to get answers from Warren. She also couldn't rely on her brothers to help with those arrangements, since she wanted them working this investigation.

Rachel stood to face her brother. "What time are Marlon's and Alma's interviews?" she asked.

"The first is at noon. The other, two hours later," Egan answered, and then he shifted his attention to their father. "Can you get to your room by yourself or do you need help?"

It was possible that Warren answered, but if so Rachel didn't hear him. That's because she felt a tingling feeling in her stomach, then saw a glowing light. Mercy, she knew what that was: an aura. And it always happened right before a seizure.

Rachel looked at Griff to tell him what was happening, but it was too late. Still, he seemed to know, because he lunged for her, catching her in his arms before she fell to the floor.

"I'M FINE," RACHEL grumbled to the doctor.

Griff didn't believe her, and obviously neither did Egan, since he gave her a big-brother stare-down. Ditto for Dr. Henry Baldwin not believing her, since he continued to examine her. He had already taken a blood sample.

"This checkup is just a precaution," Dr. Baldwin explained. He'd given her several variations of that assurance in between listening to her heart and checking her pupils.

"I've been taking my meds," Rachel went on. That, too, was something she'd been repeating since Griff and Egan had rushed her to the hospital.

Over the years, Egan had no doubt witnessed his sister having many seizures, but it still seemed to shake him up. It had certainly done that to Griff. That was in part because Rachel had said she'd been seizure-free for two years. It was always possible for an epileptic to have a seizure, but Griff definitely didn't like the timing of this one.

"Is this stress related?" he asked Dr. Baldwin.

The doctor only lifted his shoulder. "Maybe, but these things happen with or without stress. If there are any red flags, the test results might show it. *Might*," he emphasized. "In the meantime, I want her to get plenty of rest. The same for Warren. Please tell me he didn't come to the hospital with Rachel and you."

Egan shook his head. "He didn't. I insisted that he stay put."

Warren had thankfully done that, but it hadn't stopped the man from texting both Egan and Griff to get updates on Rachel's condition.

The doctor helped her to a sitting position on the examining table. Griff could tell from her slight grimace that she was exhausted. That was the usual symptom after she had a seizure. Of course, this one was worse, since she'd hardly slept the night before.

Even though she was a little wobbly, she got off the table and tried to look a lot stronger than she likely felt. She gave Griff a warning glance when she thought he might start toward her to help, but he stayed put. He also knew from experience that it wasn't a good idea to treat Rachel with kid gloves after something like this.

"I'll call you if there's anything in your test results," the doctor said, looking at the tablet that contained her medical records. "Oh, and right before you two brought Rachel in, I got back the blood work on Warren."

Rachel, Egan and Griff had already started for the door, but that stopped them.

"I'll call and tell him," the doctor went on, "but since this is a police matter, I can give you the results.

Warren was definitely drugged. Someone gave him a huge dose of Rohypnol."

That was the date-rape drug, and it explained the memory loss. However, it didn't prove why someone had given it to him in the first place. Unless...

"This was to set up Warren," Griff concluded. "Someone drugged him and drove him to that location so he'd be blamed for the car bombing." And therefore blamed for Rachel's murder.

That was the only scenario that made sense, since Griff was positive that Warren hadn't tried to kill his daughter, or anyone else for that matter. Still, who would do this, and why? There was only one person with that kind of motive.

Alma.

When Griff looked back at Rachel, he realized she was volleying glances between Egan and him. "We should go to the sheriff's office and wait for Alma," she said. "She'll be coming in soon for her interview."

Yes, she would be, but taking Rachel there definitely wouldn't give her the rest that the doctor had just ordered.

"If I go home," Rachel added, "I'll only be pacing and waiting to hear the outcome of the interview. I can pace and wait at the sheriff's office."

Egan, Griff and the doctor all huffed, but Griff knew that's exactly what she'd do. No way would

Rachel be able to relax until they had some answers. Whenever that would be.

Egan's phone buzzed, and when he glanced at the screen, he mumbled something about this being a call he had to take, and stepped out in the hall to answer it.

"You have any other questions?" the doctor asked, glancing from Griff to Rachel. Both shook their heads. "Fine, then just make her sit down as much as possible," the doctor instructed. He patted Griff's arm on the way out. "Good luck with that."

He'd need luck and a whole lot more to get Rachel to cooperate, but Griff waited until the doctor was out of the examining room before he said anything to her. "I want to focus on this case, and I can't do that if I'm worried about you."

She blinked as if surprised by his words. Maybe because she didn't want to hear that he was still worried. Or that he cared for her. Which he did.

"The odds are slim to none that I'll have another seizure today," she said, "and I can rest when I get home after the interviews." She stopped, though, and gave a frustrated sigh. "I was going to make arrangements for another place to stay."

That didn't surprise him. Rachel probably wanted some breathing space away from Warren and him. But considering the fact that he'd just rushed her to the hospital, breathing room probably no longer seemed like a smart idea.

Even though Griff didn't say a word, it was obvious she was playing out his argument in her head, because she huffed. "Fine. I'll stay one more night at the ranch if you don't give me any hassles about watching those interviews."

Griff didn't want to give in to that, but the truth was he couldn't stop her. Sure, he could tell Egan to keep her out of the observation room at the sheriff's office, but she had a right to hear what Marlon and Alma had to say. And that's why Griff finally nodded.

When they went into the hall, Egan was just finishing up his call, and he turned to them. "That was the Silver Creek sheriff. They found a dead body about five miles outside town. Male, about fifty years old, and he was killed with a single gunshot wound to the head. They think he might have been the person who set the bomb because he had some explosive paraphernalia in his truck."

"He's really dead?" Rachel asked. She made a sound of relief when Egan nodded, but there was no such relief on her brother's face.

"The truck was stolen, and the dead guy had no ID," Egan went on. He started walking toward the exit, and Rachel and Griff followed. "There was also no gunshot residue on his hands."

So he probably wasn't the man who'd tried to gun them down, and that meant there had to be two of them. Maybe more. That wasn't exactly a settling thought. Because even though this guy was dead, an-other would-be killer could still be out there.

With that reminder fresh in his memory, Griff made sure Rachel hurried when they went outside to the cruiser. He also kept watch as Egan drove to-ward the sheriff's office. Along the way, Griff up-dated Egan on his father's test results, while he also kept an eye on Rachel. She definitely didn't seem steady, but there was nothing he could do about that.

She looked at him, their gazes connecting, and for a split second he saw just how bad her fatigue was before she shut down. Of course, she couldn't turn off her emotions, because coupled with that fa-tigue was still plenty of disapproval that he was the one sitting beside her. Or at least he thought it was all disapproval.

Until she glanced at his mouth.

One quick look at her, and he saw something else. The heat. Maybe she was remembering the night they'd spent together or the fact that they'd skirted around this attraction for each other for years. Either way, she wasn't having an easy time dismissing it, because she scowled and mumbled, "Really?"

For some stupid reason, that made him smile. And it seemed to ease her scowl a bit, too. She didn't ex-actly return the smile, but she no longer looked ready to punch him. Maybe that meant they'd reached some kind of truce.

Egan pulled to a stop in front of the sheriff's office, and Griff spotted his sister, Deputy Thea Morris, in the squad room. He knew from what Egan had said earlier that she was manning the place by herself while the other deputies were out working on the investigation. But his sister wasn't alone.

When Egan, Griff and Rachel went inside, they saw Alma standing there. Griff had already met the woman. Had met her attorney, Simon Lindley, but this was Rachel's first time seeing the pair.

Alma's attention immediately went to Rachel, and the woman's mouth went into a flat, disapproving line. "You're the reason I'm here," she snapped. "Well, I don't like it, and I'm tired of you McCalls and this vendetta you have against me."

Griff was about to return some verbal fire, but Rachel stepped in front of him. "Someone tried to kill us." Her voice was surprisingly strong, considering she'd had a seizure a couple hours earlier. "It's not a vendetta. We just need to know the truth so the attacks can be stopped."

"Well, you're not going to learn the truth by going after my client," Simon protested. He volleyed his attention between Griff and Egan. "This will be the last time you drag her in for questioning. If you try it again, I'll sue you for harassment. My client has done nothing wrong."

"Where was she last night?" Griff asked, the moment Simon had finished his little rant.

"I was at home," Alma said, at the same time that Simon spoke.

"She doesn't have to answer that!"

Egan huffed. "She'll have to answer it if she wants to get out of here anytime soon. But, hey, that's your call if you want to wait around here for a couple of days for the DA and me to decide if we're going to file charges."

That put Alma's mouth in an even flatter line. "What exactly do you suspect that I've done?"

Egan lifted his shoulder. "Maybe blew up a car. Drugged a man. Shot at people. Oh, and put a bullet in someone's head."

"Murder?" Simon spat out. He hitched his thumb at Alma. "You really believe she could do something like that? Look at her. She's not a killer."

"I won't know that until I've questioned her, now will I?" Egan met the lawyer's glare with one of his own, and Egan was good at it, too.

"Fine," Simon finally snapped. "You can question Alma…" Then he stopped, his attention going to the window.

Griff immediately turned in that direction, putting Rachel behind him in case there was about to be another attack. But it wasn't a gun.

It was Sheriff Raleigh Lawton.

This was another first, for Rachel to see her half brother, but she didn't question who he was. Maybe because there was a strong resemblance between him and her other brothers.

She made a sound, a soft moan that came from deep in her throat, and she took hold of Griff's arm. Maybe because she was feeling dizzy, but it probably had more to do with seeing the proof of her father's infidelity.

"Sheriff McCord," Raleigh said in greeting when he came in. "Ranger Morris."

"Griff," he automatically corrected, though he figured Raleigh preferred to stick with the formal title. The man had certainly been keeping his distance from his half siblings.

And his father.

Raleigh nodded a silent greeting to Rachel, but his gaze did linger on her for several moments. It was as if he was studying her features, just as she was doing to him.

"I'm sorry about the trouble you had," Raleigh told her, before turning to his mother.

"Thank you for coming," Alma said. Obviously, she'd called Raleigh to tell him about the interview.

"Yes, thank you," Simon repeated. "You need to convince your fellow cop to back off."

Raleigh shrugged in that same lazy way that Egan

had just moments earlier. "Actually, I'm not here just for my mother, Simon. I'm also here because of you."

And with that, Raleigh shifted his attention from Simon to Egan. "I have some possible evidence that my mother's lawyer might have been the one who tried to kill Rachel."

Chapter Six

Rachel wasn't sure who was more stunned by Raleigh's accusation—Simon or everyone else in the squad room.

From the moment she'd seen her half brother come walking in, she'd thought he'd come to defend his mother and give them a good dressing down for "harassing" her. Instead, it was possible he was giving them their first real lead that could help them solve this case and put an end to the danger.

Well, Raleigh could be doing that *if* he actually had something.

"What the hell are you talking about?" Simon snarled. Obviously, there was no love lost between Raleigh and him because Simon gave him a look that could have frozen Texas in summer. "What possible evidence?"

The veins were suddenly bulging on Simon's neck. In contrast, though, Alma didn't seem angry. However, it appeared she was on the verge of crying. Her eyes watered.

"Sheriff Ryland in Silver Creek found a dead guy," Raleigh explained, "and when he sent out the picture, I immediately recognized him." He took out his phone, pulled up a photo of a man and turned the screen toward Simon for him to see. "I think you'll recognize him, too."

Simon took a quick intake of breath when he saw the picture. Raleigh then showed it to Griff, Egan and her. But not to his mother. Maybe because he didn't want her to see the man who was obviously dead from a gunshot wound.

"Who is he?" Griff asked.

"Dennis Gale," Raleigh and Simon answered in unison.

It was Raleigh who continued. "Dennis was a PI, and he worked for Simon."

Well, that was a connection that Simon obviously didn't want. Because it connected him not only to the dead guy but also to the car bomb.

"Dennis *used* to work for me," Simon corrected. "I fired him about a month ago."

"Why?" That question came from Griff, but Rachel figured any one of them could have asked it. Alma included, since her eyes widened a little in what appeared to be surprise.

Simon glanced around as if searching for the right

way to explain this. Of course, the right way for him would be an explanation that would no longer make him a person of interest.

"Dennis was a drunk," Simon finally said. "He botched a case where I had him keeping surveillance on a client's wife. He tried to shake down the wife for money, and in exchange he wouldn't report to me that she'd been doing some illegal things. The wife came to me, and since she had a recording of Dennis trying to blackmail her, I fired him."

"And you didn't come to me with any of that?" Raleigh snarled.

"Attorney-client privilege," Simon snarled right back. "There were things on the recording that would have violated what my client told me in confidence." He paused, muttered some profanity. "Obviously Dennis got himself mixed up in something bad."

"Yeah," Griff agreed. "Something that implicates you. Where were you last night?"

Simon's eyes narrowed. He didn't like that question aimed at him any more than he had when Griff had asked it of Alma.

"I was at work in my office until around 10:00 p.m.," he snapped. "And yes, someone saw me there. I have a cleaning service that was in the building all the way up until the time I left."

"That doesn't mean you didn't hire someone to launch the attack in Silver Creek," Griff quickly pointed out. "Someone like your former PI. Then, you could have killed Dennis when he failed to kill Rachel."

Simon cursed, and it was so raw that it caused Alma to blush. "I think you'd better go ahead and start that interview with me," she said to Egan. "I'd like to get out of here as soon as possible."

Egan glanced at Raleigh, Simon and her before he shrugged again and started walking toward the interview room. "Don't think the questions for you are over," he warned Simon. "They're just beginning."

Good. Because if Simon knew anything, then maybe her brother could figure out a way to get him to talk.

"You really think Simon could have hired a killer?" Griff asked Raleigh after the others were in the interview room.

A muscle flickered in the man's jaw. "I don't know. He hates Warren, and he's in love with my mother. That's a bad combination."

Yes, it was. "You don't happen to have financials on Simon, do you?" Rachel pressed.

"No. But I might be able to get them because of Dennis's murder." Raleigh looked at her. "Are you okay? Were you hurt in the attack?"

She felt a tightness in her chest, and it took her a moment to realize why. Raleigh's tone sounded, well, brotherly. Part of her didn't like that. She didn't want to have this man feel any connection whatsoever to her. Ditto for her not wanting to feel anything for him. But simply put, none of this was Raleigh's fault. He hadn't asked his mother and her father to have an affair, and now they were all having to live with the consequences.

"You don't have to answer," Raleigh went on, "but how's your mother?"

Again, it sounded somewhat brotherly, and while she didn't want to talk about this with Raleigh, she didn't see any reason to be rude about it, either. "She's about the same, still in the hospital." No need for her to clarify that it was a mental hospital or that her mother had had a breakdown. Raleigh almost certainly knew all that.

So that she wouldn't have to continue this conversation, Rachel was about to remind Griff that she wanted to listen to Alma's interview, but Raleigh spoke again.

"I'll let Egan know this, too, but I got a threatening email this morning." He took a piece of paper from his pocket. "I printed it out after I forwarded it to the FBI so they can try to figure out who sent it."

They'd had no luck with that so far. Whoever was emailing them was bouncing the messages off foreign servers. Still, maybe the sender had made a mistake this time and not covered his or her tracks.

Griff took the paper from Raleigh, and Rachel

moved closer to him so she could read it. The words seemed to jump right out at her: *"Sheriff Warren McCall will pay for what he's done, and that means you're going to die. I'll make sure all of his children die while he watches."*

Griff mumbled some profanity under his breath and handed the paper back to Raleigh. "That's similar to the ones we've all been getting." He turned to her then, and Rachel must have looked pretty bad because Griff cursed again and looped his arm around her waist. "I need to get her off her feet."

Raleigh nodded, and he looked as concerned as Griff did. Worse, Rachel thought there might be reason for concern because she was suddenly dizzy again. She'd never had two seizures in the same day, and if it happened, she'd almost certainly be hospitalized. No way did she want that, not with everything else going on, so she immediately tried to steady herself.

Griff led her up the hall, not to the observation room but rather to the break room, and he did just as he'd told Raleigh. He got her off her feet by having her sit on the sofa.

"You're shaking," he pointed out when he got her a bottle of water from the fridge.

She was, and it only added to her frustration. "I hate feeling weak," she mumbled. "And I hate people thinking I'm weak."

"Yeah, I know." Griff sat on the arm of the sofa next to her and brushed a kiss on the top of her head.

He did indeed know. In fact, Griff knew plenty about her since she'd poured out her heart to him over the years. And over those years, he'd actually listened.

"You just need to get some rest like the doctor said," he assured her. "And you probably need to eat something."

She did, but it wasn't her top priority. "I want to listen to what Alma is saying."

Griff no doubt wanted that, too, but he didn't budge. Probably because he knew if he got up, then so would she. "Egan will tell us if either Simon or Alma say anything we can use."

Egan would, but Rachel wanted to hear it for herself. However, she didn't want to risk wobbling again. There were already too many people worried about her, and that was only causing all of them more stress. But it was stress that she was certain Griff would understand.

"It's so hard for me to see Raleigh," she said. "Because he's proof of what my father did."

Griff nodded. "I can tell Raleigh to leave if that would help."

"No. He might have more pull with his mother than Egan does. He might get her to tell us things that she wouldn't otherwise say." Rachel paused. "But I can't stay at the house with my father. I thought I could, for another night, anyway, but seeing Raleigh…"

She didn't finish that, and judging from Griff's expression, there was no need. He knew what this was doing to her.

He dragged in a long, weary breath. The kind a person would take when he was about to say something he might regret. "It probably won't be as secure as the ranch, but I can take you to my place." He also paused. "Unless that'll just trigger more bad memories for you."

"Anyplace I go will trigger memories." Including those of the night she'd spent there with Griff.

Those memories came back now, too.

She'd spent so many years fantasizing about being with Griff that way, but Rachel certainly hadn't expected it to happen at such a low point in her life. Even then, it'd still lived up to her high expectations.

And the memories weren't going to let her forget that.

"I do have a guest room," he reminded her, probably because he wanted to assure her that a sleepover wouldn't lead to sex.

She nodded and made the mistake of looking up at him. Griff was certainly a cure for her bone-weary fatigue because all that vanished. Apparently, so did her common sense, because Rachel thought about kissing him. She thought about pulling him to her and just getting lost in his arms. It would no doubt feel good, and for a few moments she wouldn't have to think about this awful mess they were in.

However, there would be consequences.

A kiss would mean she had forgiven him, and she wasn't certain she could do that. Not today, anyway. Still, that didn't stop her from weaving another fantasy.

He dropped his gaze to her mouth, and when their eyes connected again, she saw the heat there. She figured there was no chance he'd be the one to initiate a kiss. Not after what had happened between them a month ago.

But he did.

Griff leaned down, barely touching her lips. Coming from any other man, it might have been chaste, but there was nothing chaste about Griff.

He paused, his mouth hovering over hers, and even though he didn't say anything, Rachel could feel the fierce battle he was having with himself. She was having that same battle, and was clearly losing because she didn't move away from him. She stayed put, waiting for him to continue with what would almost certainly be a huge mistake.

Griff cursed himself, and her, and got up from the sofa. "The timing isn't right for us to play with fire," he mumbled.

That was the truth. Heck, it might never be right.

That didn't stop her from feeling the disappointment, though. And that made her stupid. Because the last thing she should be doing right now was thinking about kissing Griff, and she hoped if she repeated that often enough to herself that it would finally sink in.

There was a knock at the door before it opened, and Rachel quickly tried to prepare herself in case it was Raleigh. It wasn't. It was Thea. She glanced at both of them, maybe sensing that something had nearly gone on between them. But if she did pick up on the attraction, she didn't say anything about it. Instead, she hitched her thumb to the squad room.

"Marlon Stowe just arrived," Thea said. "And he's demanding to see you."

That got Rachel to her feet. "How did he know I was here?"

"He said he's been watching the sheriff's office from the diner across the street. Yeah," Thea added, when Rachel frowned. "I thought it was creepy, too. Anyway, he claims he has to see you because he's got something important to tell you."

"What?" Rachel pressed, when Thea hesitated.

Thea frowned, too. "Marlon claims he has proof that it was your father who tried to kill you."

Chapter Seven

Griff had to mentally replay what Thea had just said before it sank in. And when it finally did register in his head, it caused him to curse. He didn't know Marlon, but Rachel had already been through enough without having to deal with this clown's accusations.

"Proof?" Griff snapped.

Thea sighed, nodded and looked at Rachel. "Of course, he's saying he'll only give that proof to you and nobody else. If you don't want to deal with him, I can arrest him for obstruction of justice—"

"No," Rachel interrupted. "I'll see him. Or rather, I'll hear what he has to say. But if this is some kind of trick, then maybe you can charge him with something. *Anything.*"

She sounded more exhausted than she looked, and that made Griff realize just how wrong that near kiss had been. Rachel definitely didn't need him adding another layer of trouble to her life.

She took some sips of water before she headed

back to the squad room. Thea stayed ahead of them, and Griff moved to Rachel's side. He also put his hand over the gun in his holster. He doubted that Marlon had come here to attack Rachel, but since the man had once had a restraining order against him, it likely meant he had a dangerous edge.

Since Marlon was also a person of interest in Rachel's attack, Griff had seen a picture of the guy, but seeing him in person was still a surprise. That's because he looked like a teenager. He wasn't. Griff knew the guy was twenty-six, but he could have passed for someone ten years younger.

"Rachel," Marlon said in greeting.

Because Griff's arm was touching Rachel's, he felt her tense. Obviously, this guy set off alarms for her, which meant he did the same for Griff.

Marlon flashed a wide smile, as if this was a social visit. However, he didn't extend that smile to Griff. "Ranger Morris. I was just doing a computer check on you while I was having coffee at the diner. Discovered some interesting things. You'd be surprised what you can learn on the internet." He motioned to the laptop bag he was carrying.

Maybe that comment was meant to intimidate Griff, because Marlon had almost certainly learned about Griff's criminal parents. But it didn't intimidate him in the least. Griff just stared him down. He also decided to hurry this conversation along.

"You have some kind of accusation you want to make against Rachel's father?" he asked.

Marlon turned back to Thea. "I said I would only talk to Rachel about this. I told you to make that clear to her."

"I didn't agree to that, and neither did Rachel," Thea insisted. "And I can promise that Griff wouldn't have agreed to it."

The man huffed, his gaze slashing to Rachel. "So, do you want to know about your dad or not?" There was no trace of that friendly tone or smile left, and Griff figured this was more Marlon's usual personality.

Yeah, the guy was definitely wound tight.

Rachel folded her arms over her chest and stared at him. "Of course I want to know, but I don't understand why we should keep it just between us. If my father truly did try to murder me, and you can prove it, then he'll need to be arrested—immediately. That means you'd end up repeating whatever you have to say to Ranger Morris and the cops."

That *wound-tight* expression went up a notch. "I thought you and I could talk privately first," Marlon pressed.

Thea had been right. No way was that going to happen, but Griff didn't even have to say so because Rachel put down her foot first.

"There's no reason for us to talk privately," she insisted. "Is there?" She didn't wait for him to answer. "The only thing I want from you is this so-called proof that you have about my father."

There was a flash of anger in Marlon's eyes before he must have remembered that Griff was watching his every move—and ready to arrest his sorry butt if he did anything wrong.

"I was hoping you'd talk to Taryn," Marlon finally said. "I want you to tell her to come back to me. I figure that won't be hard for you to do since you're the one who talked her into leaving me." There was plenty of bitterness in his voice.

Rachel shook her head. "I didn't talk Taryn into anything. I just listened to her while she cried on my shoulder."

Marlon's suddenly narrowed eyes told Griff that the man didn't believe that. Well, tough. Even if Rachel had managed to sway Taryn, that was probably the best thing that could have happened, considering what had gone on in Marlon's other relationship.

Griff huffed, put his hands on his hips and glared at the man. "You'd better not have come here to coerce Rachel in exchange for possible evidence in a murder investigation. Because if so, you'll go to jail. I'll personally see to it."

And the stare-down started. It didn't last long, though, because Marlon must have seen that Griff wasn't bluffing. No way was he letting this clown out of here before he told them what he knew.

"Fine," Marlon finally said, "but I'll need a table for my laptop so I can show you the photos."

Photos. Well, hell.

That certainly sounded like some kind of legit evidence, so maybe this wasn't just a ploy for Marlon to get back at Rachel for "interfering" in his relationship with Taryn. Griff only hoped it wasn't evidence against Warren. Even though Rachel and her dad were on the outs, it wouldn't help her mental state if Egan had to arrest the man for attempted murder. Or worse—murder. After all, there was a dead man in this, Dennis, and even though he was connected to Simon, it didn't mean he didn't have a connection to Warren, too.

Since Egan was still in the interview room with Alma, Griff motioned for Marlon to follow Rachel and him to Egan's office. Griff knew that Egan wouldn't mind, but it did make him feel uneasy when Marlon took the time to study the family pictures Egan had on his desk, wall and filing cabinet. Some were of their parents, others of Rachel and Court. Another was of Egan's late fiancée.

"Shanna Sullivan," Marlon muttered, when his attention landed on the fiancée's picture.

Rachel had obviously already been creeped out by this guy, but that had her snapping back her shoulders. "How do you know Shanna?" she asked. Except it wasn't just a simple question. It was a demand.

"Her murder was all over the news." If Marlon was the least bit concerned with Rachel's sharp tone, he didn't show it. "I remember reading the stories of how upset your brother was."

Shanna's murder during a botched robbery attempt had indeed made the news for several days, but that had happened nearly two years ago. Griff figured that wasn't nearly recent enough to stick in Marlon's mind, especially since the murder hadn't taken place near Marlon's hometown of Silver Creek. No, it was more likely that he had done intensive computer searches on Rachel, as well, and that Shanna's name had come up.

Nearly everything that came out of this guy's mouth seemed to be some kind of red flag, and Griff hated that Rachel had been under the same roof with him for nearly a month. Because she'd run from her father, it might have put her in the path of a dangerous predator. Of course, this *predator* was now trying to point the finger at Warren.

"You can set up your laptop there." Griff pointed to the edge of Egan's desk. "And while you're doing that, you can explain to me why you have this fixation with Rachel."

Marlon took out his laptop and a large manila envelope, and Griff noticed that the man had a white-knuckle grip on his computer bag. "Is that what you told him?" Marlon asked Rachel.

"No," Griff said, before she could answer. "She said you blame her for Taryn breaking up with you. But the way you're acting seems more like a fixation to me."

"Well, it's not." Marlon shifted the tense grip to his laptop and envelope when he put them on the desk. "Despite what went on between Taryn and her, Rachel's been a good customer at my parents' inn, and I'm trying to do her a favor." He stared at Griff. "Or would you rather me not give you something that would cause you to have to arrest your mentor?"

Griff was certain that tightened his own jaw. "Just show us what you have."

His reaction seemed to amuse Marlon, and Griff instantly regretted that he'd shown any emotion about Warren. Now this clown knew it was a sore spot and might try to use it.

"You should know up front that I take pictures," Marlon continued, as he pulled up a file of photos. He motioned toward the envelope. "I also printed out copies of the ones I thought would *interest* you."

Griff glanced at the file and saw that there were hundreds of photos, and judging from the quick look that Griff got, some had been taken of the sheriff's office from the diner. Apparently, Marlon had been busy while he tried to spy on Rachel.

"I took these last night," he went on, and he clicked on the first photo. "Now, before you start accusing me of anything, I hadn't planned on taking pictures of Rachel. I was just going to take some sunset shots for the inn's webpage. But about the time I started, Rachel just happened to come outside."

Well, it was indeed Rachel, and she was coming out of the inn. It wasn't dark yet so Griff could easily see her and a couple who were on the sidewalk just a few yards from the front door. Rachel seemed to be searching through her purse, and she definitely didn't have her attention on Marlon.

"I was looking for my car keys," Rachel volunteered. "I didn't see Marlon." Her voice was tight and clipped, no doubt because she didn't like the idea that someone like Marlon had been photographing her.

The next shot had her just to the edge of the camera range. The inn was in the background, and Marlon was behind her and to her right. However, Griff saw something else.

A man.

He was on the left side of the inn, and definitely not in plain sight like the couple. He seemed to be lurking behind some shrubs.

Griff pointed to the murky image. "Zoom in on that," he told Marlon.

"I've already enlarged it. And printed out a copy for you to keep."

Marlon clicked on the enlarged picture on his laptop, and even though the light wasn't that good, Griff got a look at the man's face, and it was someone he recognized. Apparently, so did Rachel.

"That's Buddy Hoskins," she said, touching her fingers to her mouth.

Yep, it was, and Griff was instantly suspicious. For one thing, Buddy was from San Antonio, a good hour away from Silver Creek. But what was more concerning was that Buddy was the one who'd supposedly sent that text to Warren to meet him at the bar. The bar where someone had likely drugged Warren.

"I know him," Rachel said. Her forehead bunched, and Griff knew why. Apparently, so did Marlon.

"He was your father's criminal informant," Marlon supplied. "I know that because I talked to him. In fact, I stopped him from following you."

She shook her head. "When did this happen? And what did he say?"

Griff wanted to know the same thing, because he was having a hard time figuring out why Buddy would have admitted to Marlon that he was a CI.

"After you got in your car and drove off, Buddy started hurrying to the parking lot," Marlon explained. "That's when I saw he'd parked a truck there." He motioned toward the envelope again. "I got a picture of the truck, too, so you could match the license plate."

Smart thinking, but the truck might not even belong to Buddy. If so, it could give them a lead as to who had sent him to Silver Creek.

"I ran to Buddy," Marlon went on, "and I demanded to know why he was there. I said if he didn't tell me, I'd call the cops, and that I wouldn't let him leave until they got there. Anyway, that's when he said he was there because Warren had hired him to find Rachel."

Rachel shook her head again. "That's not right. My father wouldn't have hired a man like Buddy, not when he has plenty of law enforcement connections."

"Maybe Warren didn't want to use those connections if he was going to do something illegal," Marlon quickly pointed out. "You know, like maybe blow up your car so you'd come running back here to McCall Canyon and to him. If so, it worked, because here you are."

Griff immediately saw a flaw with that theory. "Warren wouldn't have risked hurting Rachel just to bring her back home."

Marlon made a sound of disagreement. "She wasn't hurt. Didn't get a scratch on her from what I can see. Heck, for all I know, the shooter could have been firing blanks at her."

There weren't blanks. Griff had heard the bullets smacking into the buildings along that alley. But that led him to his next question. If Warren hadn't hired Buddy, then why had the CI been there?

"What else did Buddy say to you?" Griff pressed.

"Not much, but he didn't have to. I could see that he was fidgeting and in need of a fix." Marlon made eye contact with Griff. "I experimented with drugs when I was in college and got hooked. I've been clean for over two years now, but I know an addict when I see one, and Buddy's an addict. That's when I realized he had to be some kind of criminal informant." He paused. "Or else he was working for someone else who wanted to frame Warren."

Bingo. That was a theory that Griff had a much easier time believing. Hearing it even seemed to make Rachel relax a little.

"Still, I don't think you can rule out Warren putting all of this together," Marlon added, shifting his attention back to Rachel. "I'm sorry. That's probably not something you want to hear, but I want you to take it seriously. Despite what you think of me, I don't want you hurt."

The jury was still out on that because the third theory was that Marlon had orchestrated the attack and then arranged for Buddy, Dennis and Warren to be in Silver Creek. That way if the guilt didn't stick to Warren, Marlon could try to pin this on Simon. Either way, Griff needed to talk to Buddy.

He took out his phone and texted a fellow Ranger

to put an APB out on the man. Maybe when they found him, he would have answers to help clear this up.

"What?" Marlon practically shouted. "I don't get some thanks for doing your job for you?"

There it was. The mean streak had returned. "Thanks," Griff grumbled, but he didn't bother to put any enthusiasm into his voice. Though he was grateful. Because this gave them a new lead to chase.

One they could hopefully chase from his place, so that he could get Rachel the rest she needed.

"Thank you," Rachel added to Marlon. She didn't gush, either.

Marlon glared at her and grabbed his laptop. Griff didn't want him taking the envelope, so he snatched it up and thumbed through the contents. There were three pictures, and even though he only glanced at them, they appeared to be the same shots taken outside the inn, along with the one of Buddy's truck.

"Maybe next time when I see or hear anything, I'll just keep it to myself," Marlon grumbled.

Griff doubted that. People with fixations preferred to have contact with their targets, and because of Marlon's anger, Rachel was indeed his target. "FYI, withholding evidence is a crime," Griff warned him.

That caused Marlon to curse and move even faster in shoving the computer back into his bag. He looked ready to storm out, but he stopped and stared at Rachel. "Be careful about trusting Ranger Morris. His loyalty is to your father, not you."

Marlon was wrong about that, but Griff didn't feel especially good about it. Warren had practically raised him, and now he was going to have to investigate the man for murder and attempted murder.

"Are you okay?" Griff asked Rachel the moment Marlon was gone.

She nodded, scrubbed her hands over her arms again. "Just go ahead and call my father."

Griff would, but first he wanted a closer look at the photos Marlon had left. He knew that Rachel would, too, so he had her sit behind Egan's desk, and he laid them out in front of her. Her attention went straight to the first shot, where she was riffling through her purse.

"I can't believe I wasn't aware of my surroundings," she said under her breath. "Two men were watching me, and I didn't even notice. I was just trying to make it to the pharmacy before it closed."

Yes, and Griff had been only a few miles away. If he'd made it to Silver Creek just minutes earlier, he could have questioned Buddy and might have been able to stop the attack.

Rachel pushed aside that photo and went to the next one—the zoomed-in picture of Buddy. Griff hadn't needed to see it again to know that Buddy had indeed been watching her. What he hadn't noticed before, though, was that the side of Buddy's shirt seemed to be bulky. That probably meant he'd been armed.

Griff silently cursed. He wished that Marlon had called the cops. As close as the inn was to the Silver Creek sheriff's office, they could have been there in minutes and maybe arrested the man.

"Buddy's truck," Rachel said, when she looked at the third and final picture.

This shot wasn't nearly as clear as the other two. Probably because Marlon had snapped it in a hurry while trying to get to Buddy. It was a late model blue Ford and, thankfully, the license plate was in view. Griff was about to phone the number in when he saw something else.

Or rather, *someone* else.

A figure just at the edge of the photo. Not in the actual parking lot, but next to a tree that appeared to be a good ten yards from Buddy's truck. It definitely wasn't Warren, but it was someone both Rachel and he recognized.

Hell.

What was Brad doing there?

Chapter Eight

Brad.

The DA's name kept going through her head, and Rachel couldn't make it stop. First her father had been in Silver Creek. Then Dennis and Buddy. And now they could add Brad to the list. It was too bad Brad wasn't available to defend himself, but he hadn't answered his phone when Griff had tried to call him, and his assistant had said he was away on a business trip.

Rachel wanted to dismiss it as nothing, but she couldn't. After all, Brad hadn't mentioned that visit when he'd seen her yesterday at the sheriff's office. There was no good reason for him to hide something like that.

But there was a bad one.

If he'd been the one who'd attacked Griff and her, there's no way he would have volunteered that he had been in the area less than a half hour before someone had put a bomb on her car.

"Don't make yourself crazy over this," Griff said.

His voice was surprisingly calm, though she wasn't sure how he'd managed that. Since he could have been killed in Silver Creek, this had to be eating away at him. Plus, she knew that Griff didn't like Brad, that there was this rivalry between them. And that rivalry was because of her.

"Am I Brad's motive for the attack?" She hadn't intended to ask the question aloud, but was glad she did.

"Probably," Griff readily answered, which meant he'd already considered it. "I don't think he's as unhinged as Marlon, but Brad's always had feelings for you. Maybe he got fed up with waiting for you to return those feelings again." But then he shook his head, groaned. "And it's also possible that Brad was set up, too."

True. He could have been lured there like her father. Maybe even Buddy was, as well, and that caused her to huff.

"We can't rule out any of our suspects," she said. "Not Marlon, Brad, Simon nor Alma."

Griff made a sound of agreement and took the turn to his ranch. As he'd done since they'd left the sheriff's office, he also kept watch around them and glanced back at Thea's cruiser to make sure she was staying close. She was. Because Rachel was watching her, too, in the side mirror, she had no trouble seeing Thea.

His sister had agreed to do protection detail with him, though Rachel hated to tie up one of Egan's deputies—especially since Egan had something else to investigate. Now that he'd finished his interviews with Alma and Simon—Marlon never returned to the sheriff's office for his interview—he would need to focus on finding a money trail that would link any of their suspects to the attack. Rachel wasn't sure how easy it'd be to get financials on a district attorney, but at least he wouldn't have to start that process until he'd interviewed Brad.

Griff turned onto the ranch road, and his house came into view. Rachel had tried to brace herself for the memories that would come with seeing the place. However, it wasn't exactly memories that she got. The heat came, and the old attraction slid right through her before she could stop it.

Great. This wasn't a good start to what would be at least one overnight stay. And it wouldn't matter that Thea would be in the house with them, because Griff and Rachel would still be sharing the same space.

The very space that had landed them in bed.

He pulled to a stop directly in front of the house and got her moving inside. His golden retriever, Scout, was right there in the foyer, waiting for them, but as soon as Griff gave the dog a few rubs on the head, Scout headed off to the back of the house. She knew there was a pet door off the kitchen and that the dog spent more time outside than he did in.

Griff had a security system, and he shut the door and armed it as soon as Thea was in the foyer. She was carrying a large pizza that she'd ordered from the diner, and had her laptop tucked under her arm.

"I'll be in the kitchen if you need me," Thea said. "Help yourself to pizza if you're hungry, because I doubt there's much more than beer and sandwich stuff in Griff's fridge." She glanced at them and then seemed to hesitate a little when her attention landed on Rachel.

Rachel hoped Thea hadn't picked up on the attraction she was feeling for Griff. And while she was hoping, she didn't want Griff to pick up on it, either.

Too late.

One look at him, and she knew he was feeling things that he also shouldn't be feeling.

"Right," Thea mumbled. Her mouth quivered as if she might smile, but Griff's glare stopped that. "Don't forget about the pizza," she added, and headed to the kitchen.

"Feed Scout," Griff called out to her. "And make sure he has plenty of water."

Thea mumbled that she would and disappeared from sight. Griff's house wasn't huge, but there was a wall separating the kitchen from the foyer.

"You should eat something," Griff pointed out.

Maybe because he didn't want to talk about these feelings simmering between them.

Rachel didn't want to talk about it, either, and thankfully, she didn't have to because her phone rang, and she saw her dad's name on the screen. She needed to talk to him, to tell him about Buddy being in Silver Creek, but Rachel dreaded this conversation. Everything she'd say would no doubt seem like an accusation.

And that's exactly what it might be.

She answered the call, put it on speaker and immediately heard her father's voice. "Rachel, I'm sorry. I just now saw the missed call. I guess I fell asleep."

That could be an effect of the drug he'd been given, and she hoped his head was clearer now than it had been during their previous conversation.

"Dad, when Buddy texted you, did he say anything about going to Silver Creek?" she asked.

"No." He didn't hesitate. "I kept the text, and he wanted to meet me in San Antonio. Did he go to Silver Creek?"

"Yes, he was at the inn where I was staying, and he told the owner's son that you'd hired him to find me."

Her father cursed, something he rarely did when she was around to hear it. "No way in hell would I have hired Buddy to do something like that. He's a good CI mainly because he's a druggie rat who can't keep a secret and always needs money. But I wouldn't have let him get anywhere near you."

Rachel believed him, and that meant someone else had sent Buddy there.

"Buddy didn't answer when I tried to call him," Griff said. "Any idea where I can find him?"

"His favorite bar is a seedy place called the Moonlight on the south side of San Antonio. But if you go there, don't take Rachel. It's not a safe place."

It tightened her stomach to hear her father being so protective of her when she was still furious with him. But she couldn't expect him to stop being a father simply because he'd screwed up.

"By any chance do you remember seeing Brad anytime in the past twenty-four hours?" Griff asked.

"Brad Gandy? Why? Does he have something to do with this?"

Rachel found it interesting that her father didn't jump to deny that Brad was involved.

"He was in Silver Creek, too, and in the same area as Buddy," Griff explained. "That means they were both there when the attack happened."

It sounded as if her father bit off more profanity before it could make its way out of his mouth. "How soon are you bringing in Brad?"

"As soon as he gets back from a business trip," Griff assured him. "By any chance do you remember anything else that happened last night?"

"No. I'm sorry about that."

So was Rachel, because if her father could remember who'd given him that drug, then they'd have the ringleader. Well, maybe. It was possible the ringleader had used another patsy so they wouldn't be able to ID him or her.

"I'll let you know if Brad or Buddy gives us anything," Griff added to her father.

"Good. Make sure Rachel gets some rest."

She didn't respond to that, but did give her father a quick "goodbye" before she ended the call. She looked up at Griff as she put her phone back in her pocket. "The person behind this could consider my father a loose end. One that needs to be eliminated."

"Yeah. That's why Egan has a deputy at the ranch, and the hands have been told to be on the lookout for anyone suspicious."

That was good, but it made her feel a pang of guilt. If she'd gone to the ranch with Griff, her father would have been better protected, and Egan wouldn't have needed two deputies standing guard, one at each house. It definitely had her rethinking her pressing Griff to bring her here.

"It'll all work out," Griff said, and he brushed a kiss on her forehead. The kind of kiss he'd given her in the break room at the sheriff's office. Coming from any other man, it wouldn't have been as hot as it was.

He looked down at her, their gazes connecting, and

mercy, that sent the heat swirling again. For a moment she thought he might kiss her again. A real kiss this time. But he took hold of her arm to get her moving.

"You really should eat something," he said.

She silently cursed the disappointment she felt. Silently cursed what else she did, too. Rachel stopped and pulled him to her. She had to go on her tiptoes to kiss him, but she managed it. In fact, she managed it even better when Griff leaned down. He hooked his hand around her waist, dragging her even closer, and he deepened the kiss.

Just like that, things went from hot to scalding, and Rachel knew this had been a huge mistake. It would be hard to put up those barriers that she'd just knocked down.

Griff seemed to have some common sense left, though, because he let go of her and took a step back. His breathing was too fast. So was hers. In fact, hers was coming out in gusts, and she was light-headed. Obviously, she didn't think straight whenever she was around him.

"We can go two ways with this," Griff said. "We can forget it happened or talk about it."

She was leaning toward forgetting. If that was even possible. Still, she should try. But Rachel didn't get a chance to give him her answer because she heard the dog bark. From the sound of it, Scout was in the backyard, and that wasn't an ordinary bark. The dog sounded frantic, as if he'd spotted something that shouldn't be near the house.

"He barks at deer sometimes," Griff said, but he drew his gun. "Thea, turn off the lights," he called out to his sister, and the rooms were close enough for Rachel to see that Thea did that.

Griff did the same to the foyer light and moved Rachel to the corner of the living room, putting himself in front of her. It put him in a good position to look out the front window, but the only view she had was of his back. Once again, Griff was protecting her.

Scout continued to bark, and Rachel didn't think it was her imagination that the dog was becoming even more agitated.

"Do you see anyone?" Thea asked. She was obviously still in the kitchen. Like Griff, she was probably at the window and had her gun drawn.

"No," Griff answered. "And no vehicles came up the road, because we would have heard them."

That didn't mean someone hadn't parked nearby, though, and gotten to his ranch on foot.

"Wait," Thea said a moment later. "I think someone's by your barn."

That put Rachel's heart right in her throat, and she was about to ask Griff for his backup weapon. But there wasn't time for her to do that.

Because a shot slammed into the house.

GRIFF DIDN'T TAKE the time to curse himself for bringing Rachel to his place, even though that bullet confirmed that he'd made a huge mistake and had put her life at risk again.

Another shot came, and this one blasted through the front window. It meant the gunman was on the move, since the second one was a good ten feet from the first one that'd been fired.

"Get down," Griff told Rachel, though it wouldn't be nearly enough to keep her safe. If the shooter was using cop-killer bullets, then the shots could easily get through the wall to her.

Griff tried to hear if there was any movement outside the house. He didn't want this guy trying to break in. But he didn't hear anything.

Not even Scout barking.

Hell, he hoped that didn't mean their attacker had done something to his dog. Since Scout wasn't much of a guard dog, he might not have actually attacked the gunman, but would have continued to bark to alert Griff that something wasn't right.

Since there could be more than one gunman out there, Griff fired off a quick text to Egan. It would take him at least fifteen minutes to get to the house—an eternity when someone was trying to kill you.

The gunman fired three more shots, one after another, and each one caused his heart to race even more. They were almost certainly doing the same thing to Rachel. Maybe even something worse, and he hoped like the devil that this didn't trigger another seizure, when she hadn't even had time to recover from the last one.

Griff made sure Rachel was as far down as she could get before he moved away from her and went back to the front window. Not directly in front of it, but rather to the side. He glanced out, but before he could try to spot the gunman, another shot slammed into the window right next to him.

The glass spewed across the room, probably some of it flying in Rachel's direction. He made a quick check on her, but couldn't tell if she'd been cut.

Another shot took out more of the glass, and Griff knew he had to do something to stop this. He couldn't just stand there and let this jerk continue to rip the house apart. Griff readied his gun, leaned out from cover and fired in the direction of the shooter. He had no idea if he'd hit the guy, but at least it stopped the shots, if only temporarily.

He heard the footsteps a split second before his sister said, "It's me." Thea was crouched down as she made her way from the kitchen to the living room. "Do you have eyes on him?" she asked.

"No."

She scrambled to the other side of the window and looked out, just as the gunman sent more bullets their way. Part of Griff wanted to tell his sister to get down. He wanted to protect her, too. But Thea was a cop, and not only would she not appreciate him playing big brother, Griff also needed her as backup.

"If you give me a gun, I can help," Rachel said.

Her voice was shaking. She probably was shaking, too, but he knew her offer was genuine. However, he would pass on her helping. She was already in a dangerous enough position without putting her closer to the line of fire.

"Scout is in the kitchen," Thea said, while she took another quick glimpse out the window. "I think the gunshots scared him, because he came in through the doggy door and ran into the pantry."

Good. Maybe he'd stay there, so that would be one less thing for Griff to worry about.

Especially since he had plenty to be concerned about right now.

The proof of that was more shots coming through the window. These next bullets took out what was left of the glass. In a way that was good, since they couldn't be hit with any other flying pieces, but the reflection off the glass had probably made it a little harder for the gunman to see them.

"If we fire at him together, it might cause him to back off," Griff said to Thea.

His sister didn't hesitate. She nodded and waited for his cue. Griff didn't have to warn her to make this fast. Thea would. And maybe, just maybe, it would work.

"Now," Griff said.

Thea and he leaned out together and started shooting. Griff emptied the clip and ducked back behind cover to reload. Thea did the same, and their joint gunfire worked. For a few seconds, anyway. But the gunman just started shooting again, and Griff could see the bullets tearing through the wall right next to where Rachel was crouching.

He cursed, hurried to her and moved her behind the sofa. It was still lousy cover, which meant he couldn't wait for Egan. He had to do something now.

"Wait here with Rachel," he told his sister, and he saw the flash of concern in Thea's eyes.

However, it was much more than just a flash in Rachel's. She took hold of his arm when he started to move away from her. "You can't be thinking about going out there."

That's exactly what he was thinking. "I'll go out back and duck behind the shrubs on the side of the house. I might be able to spot this guy and take him out."

Rachel shook her head. "And he might be able to spot you first."

That was true, but anything they did right now was a risk, including staying put.

He dropped a quick kiss on her mouth, knowing

it wouldn't stop her protest or reassure her. Still, he couldn't take the time to try to make this better. The only thing that would help was to stop the guy from shooting.

Thea stayed by the window, but the shots forced her to drop down to the floor. Griff didn't tell her to be careful, but he hoped that she would be, and he raced out of the room to the kitchen. He had to take a moment to disarm the security system, since he didn't want it going off. The blare of the alarm would mask any sounds if the shooter tried to get into the house, and he definitely wanted to be able to hear something like that.

The shots continued as Griff went onto the back porch. He paused only long enough to look around and make sure no one was lurking out there, ready to gun him down. He didn't see anyone, so he hurried to the side of the porch and jumped down into the yard. Thankfully, there was a line of mountain laurels that would conceal him enough.

Well, hopefully they would.

He used the shrubs as cover as he made his way to the front of the house, then peered around the corner to the area across from his driveway. There were plenty of trees there, which made it an ideal place for a gunman to hide.

Still, there was something troubling about this attack. Thea had said she'd seen someone near the barn, and the shooter wasn't anywhere near there. Did that mean he'd run from the barn to the trees? If so, that would have been a risky move, since Thea could have spotted him. Just in case there was someone still near the barn, Griff continued to glance over his shoulder while he pinpointed the shooter's location.

Finally, he saw the gunman. Or rather, the rifle the guy was using. Griff took aim.

And fired.

He sent three bullets right at him, and just like that, the shots stopped. Maybe that meant he'd killed him, or the guy could just be on the run. Either way, at least he was no longer firing into the house.

Griff paused, listening, but kept his gun ready in case he had to fire again. He waited and watched for any signs of movement in those trees.

Nothing.

But he did hear a sound behind him, and pivoted in that direction, bracing himself for an incoming shot.

But that didn't happen.

"Don't shoot," someone said. Whoever it was had slurred his words and sounded drunk. "I'm comin' out now. And I got my hands in the air."

The man staggered out from the barn, and just as he'd said, he did have his hands raised.

It was Marlon.

Chapter Nine

Rachel forced herself to drink the tea that Ruby had fixed for her, but it tasted like dust. Probably because her stomach was still twisted in knots. In the past two days, someone had tried twice to murder her, and both times Griff had gotten caught up in the attack. This last time, so had his sister.

They could have all been killed the night before at Griff's house. And there was no guarantee someone might not try again. Because the person who'd shot at them with that rifle had managed to escape.

That certainly didn't help her stomach.

Neither did being back at the ranch with her father upstairs. But they hadn't exactly had a lot of options as to where they could stay.

Griff's house had been shot up, and there'd been no time to put together a safe house. So it had been either the ranch or sleeping at the sheriff's office. Egan had nixed the last idea because that was where they'd taken Marlon for questioning—after a trip to the hospital. The man had been either too high or too drunk to answer any questions, but Egan planned on doing that as soon as the doctor released him.

Truth was, Rachel hadn't especially wanted to be near Marlon, either. However, she had wanted answers from the man, and so far Marlon was plenty short on those. He hadn't managed to tell Griff or Egan a single thing of importance after he'd turned up by Griff's barn.

She heard footsteps coming toward the dining room, set down her teacup and automatically got to her feet. To put it mildly, she was on edge, and part of her expected the gunman to come walking in. But it was Griff. Judging from his creased forehead, he'd either gotten more bad news or else was worried about her. She probably looked as wound-up as she felt.

"Your dad seems better this morning," Griff said in greeting. "Still no memory of what happened, though."

That was too bad, but at least Griff and he were talking. Maybe Griff could spur him to recall something that would help them, especially since Marlon wasn't being any help.

"How's Scout?" she asked. It certainly wasn't the most pressing question she wanted an answer to, but it was important, since the dog had also been shaken up from the shooting.

"He's fine. I just got a text from Ian to let me know that Scout was having fun playing with his kids."

Deputy Ian Mead had taken the dog to his place for a day or two. Ian had a house in town with a big yard, and Griff had figured that would be a better place for him than the ranch, what with all the security they had in place. Plus, the hands still had to manage the daily operation of the ranch, so it was better not to put Scout in the middle of that.

"Marlon had the same drug in his system as your dad did," Griff continued a moment later. "And like your dad, he says he doesn't remember anything about the attack. He claims he doesn't even know how he got to my house."

Rachel wasn't sure she believed that. "He could have followed us from the sheriff's office, parked up the road and walked to your barn."

Griff nodded. "But he wasn't armed, and there was no gunshot residue on his clothes or hands when Egan tested him. There wasn't even a trace on Marlon."

She groaned, wishing all this could be tied up in a neat little package. One that would lead to Marlon's arrest. Apparently, that wasn't going to happen.

"Marlon could have hired the triggerman who was shooting at us from the trees," Rachel pointed out. "And the gunman could have been Buddy. Maybe he needed a fix badly enough that he was willing to kill for it."

Obviously, that wasn't news to Griff, and he quickly nodded again. "Buddy hasn't turned up yet. And the CSIs are combing that area across from my house now for anything that can give us an ID on the shooter." He paused. "It's possible, though, that he was just a hired thug, but it could have been one of our other suspects."

Yes. Either Simon, Brad or Alma. Though Rachel couldn't picture Alma traipsing around a wooded area with a rifle. As for Brad, he still hadn't contacted them so he could explain why he'd been at the inn in Silver Creek, but he wasn't the rifle-toting sort, either.

"Simon and Alma have alibis," Griff went on. "But that's because they say they were together. Alma said that Simon spent the night at her place because she was so upset after yesterday's interrogation."

So they could be lying for each other. Or one of them could have slipped out without the other's knowledge and gone to Griff's. Even though Rachel and he hadn't exactly spread it around that they were going to his house, someone could have been watching them.

"Alma did give Egan complete access to her bank accounts," Griff went on. "And she did that without a court order. He'll have the Rangers go through everything to see if there's a money trail."

It didn't sound as if there would be. After all, Alma wouldn't have just given them her accounts to examine if she'd thought there was anything to find. "What about Simon? Did he give Egan access, too?"

"No." Griff's mouth tightened. "In fact, he tried to talk Alma out of it. He claims we're all on a witch hunt and that we'll manufacture evidence if necessary."

They wouldn't, but it had to look like it to Simon, since there was now plenty of bad blood between Alma and the McCalls.

"Egan said he didn't think Alma was holding any real grudges against your dad," Griff stated. "From what he gathered from the interview, she seems to be trying to move on with her life."

That could be all for show. Still, that theory didn't feel right. If Alma wanted to get back at her former lover, why not just go after him? Or Warren's wife, so Alma could get her out of the picture?

When that last question popped into Rachel's head, a bad thought followed.

"Is there still a guard with Mom?" she asked.

"Yes. A PI I trust, Kevin Teal. I called him about an hour ago just to make sure all was well. It is. Helen was still sleeping, but the nurse will tell her that I want to talk to her. Well, the nurse will do that if your mom's having a good enough day, and then maybe Helen will call me back."

Maybe. But Rachel knew from experience that her

mother had more bad days than good. Plus, a conversation with Griff might be too much for her to handle.

"I can't go visit her," Rachel said. "Because I don't want to risk our attacker following me there. Plus, she'd see the worry on my face, and that would upset her even more."

Griff made a quick sound of agreement. "If she calls back, you can talk to her. That might help both of you."

It would. She was a grown woman, but it was still comforting to hear her mother's voice. Even if it was also a reminder that her mother was ill and might never be the same again.

Rachel hadn't really wanted to think beyond the present, but it was possible her mother would file for a divorce. And she certainly couldn't fault her for that. Still, it ate away at her to think that her mom might never come home.

Griff glanced around the room. "Where are Thea and Ruby?"

"Thea's at the back of the house, keeping watch. Two hands are guarding the front, and Ruby's in the kitchen. She fixed breakfast, if you're hungry."

He eyed the table and her unfinished cup of tea. "You're not eating?"

Rachel shook her head. "I'm not hungry yet. Maybe later, once my nerves settle a bit." She hated that her voice cracked a little. Hated it because Griff already felt bad enough about the attack without thinking she was about to fall apart. "I'll be okay," she added.

He showed no sign whatsoever that he believed that, and with a heavy sigh he went to her and pulled her into his arms. She got another of those chaste kisses on her forehead, but just the simple hug helped. Of course, it would have been better if it hadn't helped, because then she would have moved away from him. It really wasn't a good idea for them to be touching like this.

Griff eased back enough that he could look down at her and make eye contact. "Your dad's worried about you. *I'm* worried about you."

She wanted to tell him there was no need for that, that she was fine, but the lie didn't make it past her throat.

"I know," he said, brushing her forehead with another kiss. "You hate us worrying about you."

She did, but maybe she could soon convince them that she was okay. It was just that she had been thrown off-kilter with the seizure and the two attempts to murder her. It was going to take a lifetime for her to forget the sound of that explosion and those bullets.

Rachel was about to step back, but Griff spoke before she could do that. "You kissed me," he said. "Right before all hell broke loose at my house."

He hadn't needed to add that last part. She was

well aware of what kiss he was talking about. And yes, she had indeed done that.

"I'm trying very hard to remember why that kiss was such a bad idea," she replied. Though that was probably something she should have kept to herself, because it caused Griff to smile.

He had an amazing smile. One that reminded her of why she'd kissed him, and wanted him in the first place.

For a moment she thought he would back away and take that bedroom smile with him. After all, they were in the dining room, where anyone, including her father, could come walking in at any minute. But this time it was Griff who did something stupid, by leaning in and putting his mouth on hers.

Just like the other times they'd kissed, the heat came. Mercy, did it. Rachel could feel it make its way from her mouth to all parts of her body. And the heat just kept coming when he pulled her deeper into his arms.

He tasted good. A taste she had no trouble remembering. Of course, it helped that they were now pressed right against each other so she could feel the tight muscles in his chest. She also heard the deep groan that rumbled in his throat. Apparently, his brain was protesting this, but the rest of him continued with it.

Griff slipped his hand around the back of her neck,

angling her head so he could deepen the kiss. It was too much, too soon, but Rachel did absolutely nothing to stop it. In fact, she made things worse by sliding her hands around his back and inching their bodies even closer. Even though this was still just a kiss, it was beginning to feel a lot like foreplay.

He groaned again and muttered some profanity when he stepped back. She hated the feel of him moving away from her, and the kiss had so clouded her mind that it took her several moments to figure out why he had put an abrupt end to it. But even over the low roar of her pulse in her ears, she finally heard what Griff must have.

The sound of an approaching car engine.

Considering how recent the attacks had been, Rachel was stunned that she hadn't been more alert, but the vehicle had already come to a stop in front of the house.

"If there'd been a problem, the hands would have called us," Griff said, probably because he'd seen how tense she'd suddenly gotten.

That was true, but it still took a couple seconds for her to rein in her too-fast heartbeat.

Griff went to the foyer, and huffed when he looked out one of the side windows. "It's Brad."

Obviously, the hands hadn't known that Brad wasn't exactly a welcome visitor. Not anymore. But they probably hadn't heard about his change in status, since he often came to the ranch.

"Stay back until I find out if he's armed," Griff warned her.

She did. Rachel stepped into the adjacent family room while Griff disengaged the security system and opened the door.

"Where's Rachel?" Brad immediately snapped. "I need to see her."

Griff didn't budge, and in fact, he blocked Brad from coming in. "We've been trying to get in touch with you for hours. Where have you been, and why didn't you return our calls?"

"I was away on business, but I came as soon as I heard what happened. Someone tried to kill Rachel again." Brad didn't pause long enough for Griff to respond to that. "What the hell were you thinking, taking her to your place? You knew how dangerous that could be for her."

No way could Rachel stand there and let Griff take the blame for that. "I insisted we go to his house." That was close to the truth, anyway. She just hadn't wanted to come back home.

Brad tried to barge in again, but Griff pushed him back on the porch. Rachel figured this could turn ugly fast, so she went closer. However, she still didn't get near the doorway, since there could be a sniper in the area.

"Could you go ahead and search Brad for a weapon so the three of us can talk?" she asked Griff.

"The three of us?" Brad snarled. He was snarling even more when Griff patted him down. "And now you're treating me like a criminal. I'm the DA and Rachel's a close friend, or did you forget?" He added a glare at Griff with that last question.

Griff ignored him, continued the search and came up with a gun. Probably one that he took from the concealed holster that Brad usually wore. Griff put the weapon on the foyer table. "You'll get that back when you leave."

When Griff finally allowed him to come in, Brad's gaze zoomed straight to her. "What the hell is going on?" But as soon as he'd growled out that question, his expression softened. He went to her as if he might pull her into his arms, but Rachel dropped back a step. She would have dropped back even farther if she had to, because she had no intention of letting him touch her.

Brad's soft expression vanished, and he aimed another glare at Griff. "What have you been telling Rachel to turn her against me?"

"I didn't tell her anything, but we did see a picture that made us think twice about trusting you," Griff answered. He shut the door.

"A picture?" Brad questioned. "What picture?"

"One that was taken outside the inn at Silver

Creek where Rachel was staying. It was snapped the very night someone tried to kill her. Any reason you wouldn't tell us you were there?" Griff pressed. "And before you answer, remember that anything you say can and will be used against you if I decide to arrest you for withholding evidence."

Brad opened his mouth as if he might blast Griff for that, but just as quickly turned back to her. "This isn't how it looks."

Rachel folded her arms over her chest. "Then why don't you tell us what happened? Because it's looking pretty bad right now."

He nodded, but it took him several long moments and a couple deep breaths before he finally got started. "I didn't mention it because I didn't want you to think I was stalking you. I wasn't," he quickly added. "But I got an anonymous tip that you were staying there, and I wanted to see for myself."

"An anonymous tip?" Griff sounded as skeptical as she felt. Although someone had lured her father there after he'd been drugged.

Brad took out his phone. "It was a text." He scrolled through and pulled up the message from an "unknown sender." "I thought it might have come from Warren. He's always wanted Rachel and me to get back together, and I figured he gave me her location so I'd go after her and bring her home."

She looked at Griff to see if he was buying this.

He wasn't. But Rachel wasn't sure just yet what she believed. "Why would you think my father would send you a text from an unknown number?" she asked.

"I thought maybe he wouldn't want you to know that he was the one who'd tipped me off to your location. I figured he had a burner cell lying around and used it to cover his tracks."

That was a stretch, but it was possibly true. She wouldn't have wanted her father involved in any search to find her. Actually, she hadn't wanted anyone involved, because she'd wanted to stay hidden away. But at the time she would have been especially resistant to having her father, or Griff, find her. It was amazing how her perspective could change after such a short period of time.

"Why didn't you say something to me when you saw me at the inn?" Rachel pressed.

"Because I saw the other two men, and I wanted to make sure they weren't following you. I mean, your whole family was getting those threatening emails, and I didn't know if someone was stalking you."

"Apparently, a lot of people were doing just that. You, included."

Brad shook his head. "No. I just wanted to make sure you were safe. If one of those men had gone after you, I would have stopped him. But the two of them got in some kind of argument, so I left to try to see where you were going. My car was parked up the street, but by the time I got to it, you were already out of sight."

That meshed with what Marlon had told them, and Brad wouldn't have necessarily recognized either of the men. Well, he wouldn't have recognized them if he was innocent.

"What'd you do then?" Griff asked, using his lawman's tone.

Brad lifted his shoulder. "I left and came back home."

Now she was skeptical again. "You drove all the way to Silver Creek to see me and then just left?"

Brad huffed and looked away from her. "I realized how stupid it was to go there. You're a grown woman, and if you'd wanted me to know where you were, then you would have told me. It felt as if I'd violated your privacy." He glanced at Griff then. "And I figured you'd already had enough of that."

That was no doubt a dig at Griff, and it meant that Brad had perhaps heard about her going to him the night of her father's shooting. Griff ignored the dig and kept on questioning Brad.

"Did you see Warren when you were in Silver Creek?"

"No," Brad answered without hesitation. "And I saw nothing illegal going on."

Griff didn't exactly roll his eyes, but came close.

"You didn't notice that one of the men was taking pictures?"

"Of course I did. He was taking pictures of the inn, and that's when Rachel came out." Brad paused. "I don't remember him aiming the camera in my direction, though."

"He claims he was taking a picture of the parking lot and that you just happened to be in the shot," Griff explained.

Brad's eyes narrowed a little. "That guy was Marlon Stowe, the jerk who has it in for Rachel?"

Griff nodded. "That's the one. Now explain to me again why you wouldn't have told Egan or me about this little visit to Silver Creek."

"Because I knew it would look bad," Brad snapped. "There was no way I could explain it to Rachel where she wouldn't think bad of me." He turned to her again. "But I swear, I was just trying to make sure you were okay. You were so upset when you left town, and I was worried."

Brad reached for her, but as she'd done before, Rachel stepped back. He huffed and scrubbed his hand over his face. "I don't know why I bother. It's obvious that Griff's turned you against me."

"This has nothing to do with Griff." Again, that was mostly true. "And you did do something wrong. But you didn't tell the truth. This puts Egan in a very bad position, because now he's got to work with a district attorney he might not be able to trust."

"He can trust me!" His voice was practically a shout, but she could see him trying to push down his temper. "*You* can trust me. But can you say the same thing about Griff? Rachel, he nearly got you killed by taking you to his house. Please. Don't stay here with him. Let me protect you."

"No." She didn't have to think about that, either. And her response had nothing to do with that kiss. "I'm staying in Griff's protective custody."

That tightened every muscle in Brad's face. "Even after he lied to you?" He aimed an accusing finger at Griff. "I didn't tell you the truth about seeing you in Silver Creek, but Griff's lie was much, much bigger. He knew about Warren's affair and kept it secret. That's the kind of man he is."

And with that, Brad snatched up his gun and stormed out, slamming the front door behind him. Griff didn't say a word. He locked the door and went to the window, no doubt so he could make sure that Brad left.

"That's not the kind of man you are," Rachel argued. And, yes, the kiss probably was responsible for her saying that. Still, it was true. Griff wasn't a liar by nature, but she was beginning to wonder if Brad was.

Griff was still watching Brad drive away when his phone rang, and she saw the name on the screen.

Kevin Teal. That was the bodyguard at the hospital where her mother was staying.

Griff answered on the first ring and put the call on speaker. "Is everything okay?" he immediately asked.

"Everything's fine with Mrs. McCall. She's still asleep. But she just got a visitor, and I thought I'd run it past you first because he's insisting that he talk to her. The guy says his name is Buddy Hoskins."

Oh, God. Buddy was there.

"Call the cops," Griff insisted. "And whatever you do, don't let Buddy anywhere near Helen."

Chapter Ten

"I should be there at the sheriff's office when the San Antonio cops bring in Buddy," Rachel said.

It wasn't the first time she'd mentioned that in the past half hour, since they'd gotten the call from the PI at the hospital, and Griff knew it was frustrating for Rachel to be tucked away at her family's ranch while not one but two of their suspects were being brought in for questioning. SAPD was on the way to McCall Canyon with Buddy, but at this very minute the doctors were also in the process of releasing Marlon, who would also be escorted to Egan's office.

And that was the reason neither Griff nor Egan wanted Rachel there.

Either Marlon or Buddy could be the person who'd tried to kill her, and while it might give her some satisfaction to face them down, it was way too dangerous. Griff doubted that either man would attack her at the sheriff's office, but a trip there would mean being out on the road. With the sniper still at large, it was a huge risk he didn't want to take.

Griff continued to set up his laptop while Rachel paced across her office. "You'll be able to watch the interrogations," he reminded her. "Egan will text us when he's ready."

Griff was trying to link to the camera in the room where Egan would be conducting the interviews. She already knew all that, of course, but judging from the look she gave him, merely watching wouldn't be enough.

He considered playing the guilt card and mentioning that he didn't want to be shot at again today, but he didn't want to put that on Rachel. She already looked ready to drop, and that's why Griff stopped what he was doing. He took her by the hand and had her sit on the small sofa.

"Why would Buddy have even tried to see my mother?" she asked. Griff put a bottle of water in her hand, and she took a sip as if she were on autopilot.

It was a question he'd been giving a lot of thought to in the short time since they'd learned about it. Part of him wanted to dismiss it as the actions of a druggie who might not even know what he was doing. But that couldn't be right. Buddy would have had to remember Warren's wife, along with also knowing that she was in the hospital. According to Warren, the man had never met Helen, so what could he have wanted to say to her that he couldn't have said to Warren? In a simple phone call…

Yes, something about that definitely didn't make sense.

Griff was in such deep thought that it took him a moment to realize Rachel was staring at him. "Please don't keep anything from me. There have been too many secrets already."

Yes, there had been, and Griff didn't want any more. He was just now starting to tear down the walls that Rachel had put up between them, and he didn't want to do anything to ruin that. Of course, even without the walls, she still might never fully trust him again.

The kisses might have been just that. Kisses. The attraction had always been strong between them, but that didn't mean things were going to change. And Griff wasn't even certain he wanted that, because in the back of his mind he would always wonder if he was good enough for her. Old baggage was a bear when it came to relationships.

"This isn't much of a secret because I told you I was going to let your father know about Buddy trying to see your mother, but Warren asked to watch Buddy's interview," Griff said. "That means he'd have to be in the office with us. He'll understand if you say no."

She stared at him, then gave a heavy sigh. "Let

him know it's okay. He might see something in the interview that'll help with the investigation."

That was Griff's take on it, too, so he sent Warren a text to let the man know he could come to Rachel's office. She stood, looking as if she was trying to steel herself for this. What she didn't do was sit behind her desk, nor had she the entire time they'd been in the room. Instead, she went to the bookcase, which was chock-full of family photos.

There was a tap at the door. Warren, no doubt. But he didn't come in until Griff opened it for him.

"Thank you," Warren immediately said.

Rachel didn't look back at her father when he came in. She kept her attention on the photos. There were some old pictures of Egan, Court and her as children. Another of Griff and her after he'd just become a Ranger. There was also a picture of Rachel with some of her former coworkers at social services, where she'd once worked. That was four years ago, before she'd taken over as ranch manager.

"I'll probably go back to my job as a social worker," she said. She gave another sigh. "Well, I will when someone stops trying to kill me."

"If that's what you want," Griff settled for saying. He looked at Warren to see how he was handling this. Not well, but then her dad must have known it was a strong possibility that Rachel wouldn't want to keep working for him.

"I can't stay here. I can't do this." Rachel tipped her head toward the desk, then finally made eye contact with her father. "This isn't about punishing you. It's just what I need."

He nodded, ran his hand over his head and nodded again. "All right. I'll see about getting some help in here. Any objections to Rayna coming in?"

Rayna would almost certainly be Warren's daughter-in-law soon, since she was engaged to Court. She was also a good choice since she was in the process of moving her horse training operation to the ranch.

"I think Court and Rayna would like that," Rachel said, and there wasn't a trace of bitterness in her voice.

For Warren, that lack of bitterness was probably not a good thing. If Rachel had been speaking out of anger, he could hold out hope that one day she would get past what he'd done and come home. But whatever she was feeling was a few steps past the bitterness stage, and she was clearly making plans for the future.

Plans that might not include any of them.

Griff's phone dinged with a text message from Egan. "Buddy's in the interview room," he relayed, and that sent the three of them to his laptop. "Egan has Marlon in another room, and he'll question him when he's done with Buddy."

The moment Griff had the feed turned on, he saw Buddy already seated at the table. The man was hunched over, his elbows on the tabletop, his hands pressed to the sides of his head.

"Can Buddy hear us?" Rachel whispered.

Griff shook his head. "It's a one-way feed for both the camera and audio. Buddy knows he's being recorded, though." And Griff hoped that didn't cause the man to hold back any information that could incriminate him.

"You've agreed to talk to me without your attorney present," Egan reminded Buddy the moment he walked into the interview room.

"Yeah, yeah." The man wasn't slurring his words, but he did seem agitated and hungover. "Let's just finish this so I can get out of here. Last I heard it's not a crime for a man to go to the hospital to visit someone."

"That depends on what you planned to do if you got in to see my mother," Egan snapped. From the sound of it, he was agitated, too, but then he was probably working on caffeine and adrenaline.

"Well, I wasn't planning on hurtin' her if that's what you're thinking." He groaned, pressed his hands even harder to his head. Since Buddy was a junkie, he was likely in need of a fix. "I just wanted to ask her some questions, that's all."

"What questions?" Egan demanded.

"I just want to know what's going on."

Egan pulled back his shoulders. "That's exactly

what I planned on asking you. Now start talking. And FYI, Helen McCall isn't the one with answers about any of this, so in the future, you stay away from her. Got that?"

"Yeah, I got it." Buddy mumbled something under his breath that Griff didn't catch. "But I don't have answers, either. I don't know what the hell's going on, but I figure it's something bad or I wouldn't have been dragged in here to the sheriff's office."

"You're right about it being bad," Egan confirmed. "And it's going to get a whole lot worse for you if you don't start talking. For starters, why did you text my father and ask him to meet you in San Antonio two nights ago when you were actually in Silver Creek? And before you say that you weren't there, we have this." Egan took out the photo of Buddy in the parking lot at the inn.

He picked up the picture, stared at it for a moment and shook his head. "Yeah, I was there. Warren sent me a text asking me to check out the place. He said his kid was staying there, and she might have crossed paths with somebody bad."

"I didn't do that," Warren insisted. "I wouldn't have done that. I didn't even know where Rachel was."

Griff believed him, and judging from the look Rachel gave him, she did, as well. "Is Buddy capable of setting up an attack and an explosion?" she asked her father.

"No." Warren seemed pretty certain about that. "The bombing and the shooting were part of an organized plan, and Buddy's anything but organized."

Griff couldn't argue with that, and while they could possibly rule out Buddy, they still didn't know who was behind this. If Buddy couldn't tell them, then maybe Marlon could.

"Two nights ago, did you send Warren a text to have him meet you at a bar in San Antonio?" Egan asked, continuing with the interview.

"No," Buddy answered, but then he hesitated. "Maybe. I honestly don't remember. Sometimes I forget things."

Yeah, probably when he was wasted. Maybe that's what had happened. But Buddy could be concealing the truth because it would make him an accessory to attempted murder. Or even murder.

Buddy had another look at the picture, and his brows drew together. "Who took this?"

"You don't remember?" Egan asked.

Buddy kept studying it. "Was it that Marlon fella? The one who works there?" Then he cursed, and didn't wait for Egan to respond. "It was him, wasn't it? That little nitwit's trying to set me up."

That got Griff's attention. Apparently, it got

Egan's, too, because he immediately fired off another question. "How exactly is Marlon trying to do that?"

Buddy cursed some more. "I don't know, but he's a meth head with a mean temper. He must have wanted me there in his town to set me up for something."

"You know Marlon well?" Egan said, taking the question right out of Griff's mouth. Considering the sounds of surprise Warren and Rachel made, this was news to them, too.

"I know him," Buddy spat out. "I used to help him get his stuff every now and then, but we had a parting of the ways when I quit doing that sort of thing. It was too risky, and I didn't want to go back to jail."

"Marlon never mentioned that he knew Buddy," Rachel said. "He told us that he guessed Buddy was a CI, and made it seem as if that night was the first time he'd ever seen Buddy."

Marlon had indeed said that, and now Griff tried to think of a reason why Buddy would lie. He couldn't think of one, but could certainly come up with a reason for Marlon lying. No way would he tell the truth if he was the one behind these attacks.

"Now I'm thinking that maybe Warren didn't send me that text to check on his kid," Buddy went on. "Maybe it was this idiot Marlon." He groaned. "He sent me a text to get me there so he could set me up, didn't he? He planned for me to take the fall for what nearly happened to Warren's kid and that Texas Ranger."

Rachel pulled in a breath and placed her palm on her chest as if to steady her heart. "Marlon is bad news," she whispered. "He wants to get back at me for what happened with his girlfriend, and what better way to do it than to set up his former drug supplier, who also happened to be my father's CI?"

Buddy would indeed make a good patsy, and Griff wasn't surprised when Egan excused himself from the interview and stepped out of the room. A moment later, Griff's phone rang with a call from him.

"You heard?" Egan asked.

"Every word. You believe him? Because I certainly do."

"Yeah, I believe him, and that's why I'm going across the hall now to talk to Marlon. I'd rather not wait until we can set up a feed from the camera to your laptop, so I'll just have to let you know what Marlon says."

Griff thanked him, ended the call and turned back to the screen. Buddy was on his feet now, shaking his head and mumbling under his breath. Obviously, he was becoming even more agitated. That went on for a couple of seconds before he threw open the interview room door and stormed out into the hall.

"I wanna talk to that meth head now!" he shouted. He added a lot of curse words. "You lied. You made the cops think I was in Silver Creek to kill somebody, and you know that wasn't true. I was set up."

The camera angle wasn't wide enough for Griff to see Egan or Buddy, but he had no trouble hearing them. Or Marlon.

"What's he doing here?" Marlon snarled. His voice wasn't as loud as Buddy's, but it was close.

"You set me up," Buddy repeated.

"You stay the hell there," Egan interrupted, and a moment later, Griff saw him putting Buddy back in the doorway of the interview room.

Now Griff could see not only Egan's face, but Marlon's, too, and Marlon was not a happy camper. His eyes were narrowed, and every muscle in his face was tight.

"I didn't do anything to you," Marlon insisted. "You just showed up in Silver Creek, where I happen to live."

"Buddy says you know him," Egan told Marlon. "It's true?"

Marlon took his time answering that. "Yeah. I met him when I was using, but until the night before last, I hadn't seen or spoken to him in two years."

"You sent me a text to lure me to Silver Creek," Buddy snapped.

"No, I didn't." Marlon turned to Egan and repeated that. "And I didn't mention that I knew Buddy because I didn't think it was important. What was im-

portant was that he was there spying on Rachel and
that he was up to no good."

The accusation caused Buddy to try to launch
himself at Marlon, but Egan put a quick stop to it.
He practically shoved the man back into the interview room.

"You need help?" someone asked. Court. He made
his way up the hall toward them.

Egan gave a quick nod. "Make sure Buddy doesn't
come out. I'll finish the interview with him when I'm
done with Marlon."

Even though he wouldn't be able to see or hear
Egan in the interview room with Marlon, Griff hoped
that Buddy would say something else that would help
them unravel what was happening. However, Rachel's
phone rang before Court could get Buddy seated.

"It's Dr. Baldwin," she said, looking down at the
screen.

Since he was the doctor who managed her seizures, Griff hoped nothing was wrong. Obviously,
Rachel thought that was a possibility, because she
stared at the screen a moment longer, as if dreading
to hear what he might say.

"I'll be right back," she added to Griff and Warren, and went into the hall to take the call.

"Is she okay?" Warren asked, keeping his eyes on
her until she closed the door behind her.

"I don't know," Griff answered honestly. It obviously wasn't what Warren wanted to hear. He had enough to worry about, but Griff could tell that he'd just added his daughter to his worry list.

Griff intended to stay put and respect her privacy, but when he heard Rachel gasp, he opened the door to check on her. Seeing her didn't help relieve any of his worries. That's because there wasn't a drop of color left on her face, and without saying a word, she handed him the phone.

"Dr. Baldwin? It's me, Griff. What's wrong?" He wasn't sure he was ready to hear what had caused Rachel to react that way, but since she looked ready to slip to the floor, he hooked his arm around her waist, and he put the call on speaker.

"I'm not sure I should be the one to tell you," the doctor said. "That should come from Rachel."

"Tell him," Rachel insisted.

Even with that order, Dr. Baldwin hesitated several moments. "When you brought Rachel to the hospital, I had some tests run. Well, I just got back the results." The doctor paused again. "Rachel's pregnant."

Chapter Eleven

Pregnant.

Rachel kept repeating the word to herself, but it didn't make sense. Apparently, Griff was having a similar reaction, because he looked as stunned as she felt. And she was confused, too. Because there was something about this that didn't make sense.

"The test results must be wrong," she told Dr. Baldwin. "I took a home pregnancy test two weeks ago, and it was negative."

Judging from the look of shock that went through Griff's eyes, he hadn't had a clue about the test. But then, they hadn't exactly had a chance to discuss something like that.

"Were you having symptoms?" the doctor asked her. "Is that why you took the test?"

"No. No symptoms. I just, uh, wanted to be sure."

"I would ask if you're having symptoms now, but with all the stress you've been under, you might not have even noticed if you were. Anyway," he continued, "home pregnancy tests are reliable, but not as reliable as the test I had done. I can repeat it, of course, but with everything that's going on in your life, I didn't think you'd want to leave the ranch."

Dr. Baldwin didn't seem especially hopeful that there'd be a different outcome if she took a second test, but Rachel had to know for sure. "Is there any way you can have someone bring a test kit here?"

"Of course. But if it's positive, I'll need to examine you again, because we might need to adjust your seizure meds."

Oh, mercy. She hadn't even thought of that. The possibility of a pregnancy didn't seem real, but if it was, there was no way she would want the meds to affect the baby.

"What should I do?" she asked, and tried not to sound as if she was about to cry. That's because Griff had his attention pinned to her, and she could see both the worry and the guilt written all over him.

He was blaming himself for this.

"Just stay put. I'll have a medic bring you another kit," the doctor stated. "It'll probably be similar to the one you took two weeks ago. You'll get a quick result. I'll also have the medic get a blood sample from you, and I can have that tested in the lab."

He ended the call, and Rachel just stood there for several long moments, staring at her phone after she took it from Griff. She was too stunned to think of anything beyond redoing the test, but reality soon started to sink in. It was obviously doing the same for Griff, because she heard him groan. Then, she saw the apologetic look in his eyes.

"Don't," she warned him. "I'm not going to let you put the blame for all of this on your shoulders. No one forced me to get in bed with you."

"No, but you weren't thinking straight."

That was the truth, but it also stung. Because it made it seem as if she'd been with him only because she'd been out of her mind. But the truth was she'd always been attracted to Griff, and that night had been no different.

"Let's just wait until I repeat the test," she said. Rachel also glanced over Griff's shoulder to see if her father had heard any of this. His back was to them, his attention still focused on the computer screen. If he'd heard anything, he wasn't showing any sign of it.

Good.

She needed to process this before she had a conversation about it.

A baby.

That sent emotions slamming through her. She'd always wanted children, but the timing couldn't be worse. Even though things were improving between them, Griff and she were still at odds. And that wasn't the biggest problem. There was someone trying to kill them, and if she got hurt in an attack now, a baby she carried could be hurt, as well.

"You need to sit down," Griff whispered to her.

He put his arm around her and started walking. Not toward the office, but rather to the family room. He had her sit on the sofa, and she didn't stop him from giving her the kid-glove treatment, because her nerves were tangled and raw.

His phone dinged with a text message, and even though Rachel knew it could be important, she didn't move so she could see the screen. In fact, she wasn't sure she could move, and the bad thoughts came. Not just of their attacker, but also her seizure meds. She wasn't sure they should be taken during pregnancy. And then there was the seizure itself. That couldn't have helped, either. Sweet heaven. She needed to ask Dr. Baldwin about that, too.

Griff disappeared for a couple seconds, then came back with a glass of water. "That was a text from Egan," he said. "He's going to have to let both Marlon and Buddy leave."

Since Egan didn't have enough concrete evidence against either of the men, she'd expected that, but the news still twisted away at her. Buddy and Marlon were suspects, possibly both very dangerous, and as long as they were at the sheriff's office they weren't a threat. But now they'd be back on the street, where they could plan another attack. Of course, they might not have to do any planning if Simon was the one behind this.

She had a long drink of water and looked at Griff from over the rim of the glass. "You could fix yourself something stronger." Rachel tipped her head to the bar in the corner of the room.

He shook his head. "I'm okay."

"Liar." Nothing about his expression or body language indicated that he was okay. In fact, Griff possibly looked worse than she did, and Rachel passed him the glass of water. "Don't worry. If I really am pregnant, just know you don't have to do anything."

A new emotion went through his eyes. Anger. "Yes, I do." He gulped some of the water as if he'd declared war on it. "You think I'd let you go through something like this on your own?" He didn't wait for her to answer. "Because I would never abandon my child. *Never.*"

Only then did she realize she'd hit a nerve. His own parents had basically abandoned Thea and him, and even though Griff rarely spoke about it, that abandonment had cut him to the core. It had also left him struggling to try to fit in. Warren had helped with that. Some. But there was probably nothing that would make Griff forget the feelings of being unwanted by his own father.

"I'm sorry," she said. "I just didn't want you to feel trapped or anything."

Anger flashed through his eyes again, but he didn't get a chance to respond to that because his phone rang. It wasn't Egan. This time it was her mother's bodyguard, Kevin Teal, and it gave Rachel a new jolt of concern that something else might have happened at the hospital.

Griff answered right away, and even though he hesitated, he put the call on speaker. He was probably debating if he wanted her to hear this. She did. But if it turned out to be more bad news, Griff no doubt would have preferred to give her a toned-down version.

"Griff, I thought you'd want to know that Mrs. McCall just called Alma Lawton and asked to meet with her. Alma agreed. Neither her doctor nor I could talk her out of it. Her doctor definitely doesn't think this is a good idea."

Rachel didn't think so, either. She groaned and took out her phone so she could call her mother, but stopped when the bodyguard continued.

"Alma's on her way here now," Kevin said. "And she's not alone. She said she'd be bringing her lawyer, Simon, with her. Griff, I think it'd be a really good idea if you got here right away."

GRIFF TRIED TO FOCUS. Hard to do, though, with all the thoughts flying through his head. Well, one specific thought, anyway.

The baby.

Rachel could be pregnant. He kept emphasizing the *could be* part of that, but the doctor hadn't seemed to think this was a false alarm. Still, Rachel and he needed to wait for the test to be repeated. Of course, there'd be a delay with that, since they were on their way to the hospital in San Antonio.

It was this trip that Griff knew should have his full attention, and that's why he kept trying to shove the idea of a baby to the back of his mind. He needed to keep watch to make sure someone wasn't following them to launch another attack. Besides, it wasn't as if Rachel and he could discuss the pregnancy, anyway, while Thea drove them in the cruiser. Since Rachel hadn't volunteered anything about this to her father or his sister, Griff would keep it to himself, too.

But he wasn't having much luck keeping it out of his thoughts.

A baby. He wondered just how long something like that would take to sink in. And just how hard this would be on Rachel. She was already dealing with too much right now, and this certainly wouldn't help. The pregnancy alone would have been enough pressure, but the fact that it was his child would only add to it.

And if there was a baby, it was his. Griff had no doubt about that.

And that would give Rachel some new baggage. After all, the child would have been conceived while he was still keeping her father's secret. That was the same as lying, and he was still trying to rebuild her trust after he'd done something like that. The distrust wouldn't help right now, because she might not want him to be part of her or the child's lives.

That wouldn't stop him from being a father, though. A real father.

Griff continued to keep watch. Rachel was doing the same. Both were making sweeping glances all around them, and at the end of one of the glances, their gazes connected. Even though she didn't say anything, Griff recognized the shell-shocked expression. Probably he looked the same.

"It'll be okay," he said. He'd been repeating that a lot lately, and Rachel didn't seem to believe it any more now than she had the other times.

The corner of her mouth lifted in a smile. Definitely not from humor, though. She started to say something, but then shook her head. "You're sure Kevin will call you if Alma and Simon try to get into Mom's room before we arrive?"

She already knew the answer to that was yes. Griff had spelled out to Kevin that no matter how much Helen insisted, Alma and Simon would not be allowed into her room. The reason for that was simple. Simon was a suspect, and Griff didn't want him anywhere near Rachel's mom unless he was there with her. And as for Alma, well, Griff couldn't see anything good coming out of a conversation between Warren's wife and his mistress.

"They'd better not upset my mother," Rachel added in a mumble.

That could very well happen. If Rachel couldn't talk Helen out of seeing Alma, then the visit might happen no matter how much everyone protested.

Rachel glanced behind them again, and while Griff knew she was looking for an attacker, she was also no doubt making sure her father wasn't following them. From the moment Warren had heard that Alma was going to the hospital, he'd wanted to be there, as well. But since Helen had repeatedly refused to see him, that wasn't a good idea, so Rachel had nixed it.

That didn't mean Warren would stay put at the ranch.

Griff only hoped if the man did leave, he would at least take a couple of the ranch hands with him. After all, threatening letters and emails had been sent to Warren, too, and he could possibly become the target for the attackers.

But that didn't feel right.

This felt more personal. Of course, both Brad and Marlon had personal connections to Rachel. Simon was a different story, and maybe Griff would get a chance to talk to the lawyer when they were at the hospital. Which shouldn't be long at all now, because

Thea took the final turn into the parking lot and pulled to a stop directly in front of the hospital doors.

"Stay here with the cruiser," Griff told his sister. He didn't want anyone tampering with it.

Court was already there by the door, waiting for them, since he'd had a shorter distance to drive. He came out to stand guard while Griff hurried Rachel inside.

"Are Alma and Simon here?" Rachel immediately asked her brother.

Court tipped his head to the waiting room, and Griff spotted them. Simon was pacing while talking on the phone, and Alma was seated with her hands in her lap. They weren't alone. There were six other people in the area, and Griff gave each one an uneasy glance. None of them looked like would-be killers, but anyone could be carrying a concealed weapon.

Hell. He hated bringing Rachel here.

"Mom's still insisting on seeing them," Court explained, "and Alma's still insisting on seeing her."

Rachel sighed. "Let me talk to Mom."

She started walking toward the elevator, and Griff and Court stayed right with her. But they'd gone only a couple yards before Alma got to her feet and headed in their direction. Griff had hoped Rachel could avoid a confrontation with the woman, but they seemed to be on a collision course.

"Rachel," Alma said to her.

"Mrs. Lawton." Rachel dragged in a deep breath. "You shouldn't be here. My mother is not mentally strong right now, and seeing you could set back her recovery."

Alma nodded without hesitation. "That's why I was surprised when she called and asked me to come."

Griff looked at Court to see if that was true, and he nodded. What the heck had Helen been thinking?

"I don't especially want to see Helen," Alma went on. "I mean, she's the wronged woman in all of this. I had an affair with her husband."

"Why did my mother want to talk to you?" Rachel pressed.

"She said she wanted my side of the story." Alma paused. "If she'd sounded bitter or angry, I would have said no. But she sounded broken." She glanced away, her mouth quivering a little. "I understand a lot about that. When Warren and I parted ways, I was not in a good place. If someone could have given me answers, I would have wanted to hear what they had to say."

"There's no answer you can give Helen that will help," Griff assured the woman. He braced himself in case Rachel objected to his interference, but she kept her attention on Alma. "However, just about anything you say to her will hurt."

"I'm asking you to tell my mother that you've

changed your mind, that you can't see her," Rachel said to Alma, and there was just as much emotion in her voice as there had been in the other woman's.

And speaking of emotion, Simon ended his call and practically stormed toward them. "I hope you're not harassing my client," he snarled.

"No, they're not," Alma said, before any of them could answer.

The lawyer flinched and narrowed his eyes at Griff. "What did you say to her?"

"The truth, that she should go home," Griff answered, but he also kept watch around the waiting room.

"That's not for you to say. For any of you to say," Simon insisted, sparing Court and Rachel a glare. "If Mrs. McCall wants to see Alma, then she will."

Griff was instantly suspicious. "Why would it matter to you whether or not Alma sees Helen?" And he hoped like the devil that it wasn't so Simon could get into Helen's room and carry out some kind of sick revenge against Warren and his family. If that was the case, the lawyer would never admit to it.

Simon hiked up his chin. "I think a good air-clearing is exactly what we need. What Alma needs," he amended. "Warren pursued her in their relationship, and Helen should know that."

Alma took hold of his arm. "No. She shouldn't." She looked at Rachel. "I'm sorry about coming here. I thought it would be a good thing if your mother talked to me, but I can see I was wrong." With her grip still on Simon, Alma started to walk away.

The lawyer immediately started to protest, but Alma kept moving. Because Griff had his attention on the doors, he saw the man walk in.

Brad.

"What the heck is he doing here?" Rachel asked, taking the question right out of Griff's mouth.

Griff didn't know the answer to that, but he stepped in front of Rachel. Brad noticed the move, and he frowned.

"Relax," the DA growled, and he looked past Griff at Rachel. "I got here as soon as I could." He tipped his head toward Alma and Simon, who were leaving through the hospital doors. "I see you told them to get lost. Good. I came here to do that for you."

Rachel moved to Griff's side and stared at Brad. "How did you know they were coming to see my mother?"

"I have a friend who works here," Brad readily admitted. "I asked her to keep an eye on Helen for me."

Rachel huffed. Griff did more than that. He cursed. Because it wasn't Brad's place to do something like that without telling the McCalls.

"Why would you do that?" Rachel demanded.

He looked at her as if the answer was obvious. "You've had so much trouble lately that I thought you'd want an extra pair of eyes on your mother. Especially since someone's doing their damnedest to try to kill you." He shot Griff a glance to let him know he blamed him for that.

"I don't want your friend watching my mother. We have a bodyguard to do that," Rachel said, and she turned to Griff. "Could we leave now?"

That surprised him, because Griff had been certain that Rachel would want to see her mother. And that meant something was wrong. He slipped his arm around her waist, and that's when he felt her trembling.

"I'm dizzy," she whispered to him.

Well, hell. At first he thought she might be on the verge of another seizure, but if she was, she wouldn't be asking to leave the hospital. No. This might be pregnancy related.

"You'll explain to your mother that Alma can't see her?" Griff asked Court.

Her brother nodded. "Just go ahead and get Rachel back home. She looks like she's about ready to keel over. Should I call Dr. Baldwin and tell him you need another exam or something?" he added to Rachel.

"No." She answered too fast. So fast that it caused Brad's attention to snap toward her. The DA studied her. Not just her face, either. He glanced at her stomach.

Great. Now Brad was suspicious. Griff didn't mind

him knowing that Rachel might be pregnant. It could get the man to back off from trying to have a relationship with her. But Rachel wasn't ready for anyone to know just yet.

"Be careful," Brad said to her, and it sounded a little like a warning. Probably a warning for her to be wary of Griff.

Ignoring Brad and his comment, Rachel kissed her brother goodbye, and Court followed them back to the entrance. As he'd done when they'd arrived, he stood guard while Griff and she got into the rear seat of the cruiser. Brad stayed back, but he continued to stare, or rather, glare, as Thea drove away.

"Brad is in love with Rachel," Thea mumbled under her breath as she glanced back at the man.

Yes, he was. Or maybe it was more like an obsession. For years, Warren and Brad had pressed the notion of Rachel marrying the DA, and now that it was pretty clear that wasn't going to happen, maybe Brad just couldn't accept it.

"Uh, is something else going on that I don't know about?" Thea asked. His sister was looking at him in the rearview mirror.

"No."

Griff said it at the same moment that Rachel answered, "I'm just worried about my mom."

Thea shrugged and made a *suit-yourself* sound, and got onto the road that would eventually take them back to the interstate. It had two lanes, with traffic going in both directions. That meant he needed to keep watch not only behind them, but ahead, as well.

As Griff had done on the drive down, he glanced around and immediately spotted something he didn't like.

A dark-colored truck that pulled out of the hospital parking lot behind them.

It was probably nothing, he told himself. After all, this was a busy area, since it was the route to the hospital and other businesses, but there was something about the vehicle that put a knot in his stomach. In part it was because the driver was speeding. This was only a thirty-mile-per-hour zone, and the truck was doing more than that, catching up with them.

Rachel must have picked up on his sudden concern because she turned in the seat, looking to see what had captured his attention. "Is something wrong?" she asked.

He wanted to say no, to assure her that everything would be okay, but he couldn't do that. The truck sped up even more, closing the already short distance between them, and it quickly became apparent that the driver wasn't going to stop.

"Watch out!" he told Thea.

But his warning was already too late. The truck slammed into the back of the cruiser, and the jolt sent them into the other lane. From the corner of his eye, Griff got just a glimpse of the oncoming SUV before it slammed into them.

Chapter Twelve

Rachel had no idea what had happened, but she certainly felt it. One second she was on the seat, and the next she was slung forward. The seat belt stopped her from slamming into the back of the driver's seat, but the tight snap of the strap also knocked the breath out of her.

And that's when she saw the SUV.

Or rather, what was left of it. The front end was now crumpled onto the cruiser.

Almost immediately steam started to spew from the busted radiators, making it nearly impossible to see in front of them. Behind them, though, was the truck that had caused the collision, ramming into them. Rachel prayed that had been an accident, but judging from the way Griff drew his gun, she doubted it.

No. This couldn't be happening again. This couldn't be the start of another attack. The two others had been terrifying, but this one was even worse.

Because the danger could now extend to her baby.

If she was indeed pregnant, her child could be hurt. Or worse. And that might happen when she still didn't know who was trying to kill them.

"Are you okay?" Griff asked her.

Other than fighting to catch her breath, Rachel thought she was all right, and thankfully, Griff didn't seem to be hurt, either. But she couldn't say the same for Thea. Griff's sister was moaning, maybe in pain, or maybe, like Rachel, she was having trouble breathing.

Rachel unhooked her seat belt so she could lean forward and check on Thea, but Griff pushed her right back down. And not just in a sitting position. He made sure her torso was flat on the seat.

"There could be a gunman in the truck," he warned her.

Rachel was in shock, but also filled with adrenaline. Mercy. If there was a gunman, they were trapped. Worse, the person or persons in the SUV could be in on it. Or maybe they were innocent bystanders about to be caught in the middle of a gunfight.

"Call Court and get him out here," Griff told Rachel.

Even though her hands were shaking hard, she managed to get out her phone and press her brother's number. "It went straight to voice mail," she relayed to Griff.

He cursed, but she held out hope that Court hadn't been attacked, too. She knew from experience that there were plenty of dead zones for cell service in the hospital, and that might be why he hadn't answered. She sent him a text, praying that he would get the message and respond. Fast.

From the front seat, Thea groaned again, and Rachel saw the woman lift her head. She looked back at them, the realization of what had happened registering in her eyes. Like Griff, she drew her gun. Thea also called San Antonio PD for backup.

Good.

Rachel prayed that it wouldn't take them long to arrive. This could have been just an accident, but with everything else that had gone on, she had trouble holding on to that hope.

"Can you see who's in the truck or SUV?" she asked.

"No," Griff answered. "Just outlines behind the tinted windows, but it looks like there's just one person in the SUV. Can't tell about the truck, but I think there are two of them." He paused. "I doubt it's a good sign that no one's gotten out."

No. That meant they were either hurt or else waiting to open fire on them while they were basically trapped there.

Rachel lifted her head just a fraction so she could see out the side mirror. There were already other sounds of chaos. People hitting their brakes, probably to avoid crashing into the smashed vehicles. Someone yelled out that he was calling an ambulance. The person who did so likely thought the officers inside the cruiser had been badly hurt, since Thea and Griff were staying put inside.

Praying, Rachel continued to watch, and saw the driver of the truck lower the window. So whoever it was, he was at least alive.

And then she saw the gun.

Griff pushed her flat on the seat again, and she braced herself for the shot to come. And it did.

But not at them.

One bullet, then another, slammed into the windshield of the SUV.

Sweet heaven, what was going on? Was it possible that Griff and she hadn't been the target, after all?

"Put down your weapon now," Griff shouted to the truck driver.

Whoever it was didn't listen. He fired two more shots, both of them into the SUV.

"I can't shoot back," Griff mumbled, making that sound like profanity. "There are too many people around."

There were no more shots, but Rachel heard something else. The squeal of tires on the asphalt.

"Hell, he's getting away," Griff snarled.

Thea shook her head. "I can't go after him. The cruiser engine is busted."

Rachel lifted herself up again to have another look. Yes, the truck was indeed leaving the scene. The driver had turned around in the middle of the road and was heading back in the direction of the hospital. That gave her a new jolt of fear. What if the shooter went after her mother? Just in case that was the plan, she sent off a warning text to Court.

There was the howl of police sirens, and Rachel knew it wouldn't be long before the San Antonio cops arrived. An ambulance, too, because Thea would need to be checked out, and so would whoever was in the SUV.

"The driver of the SUV's getting out," Thea said.

Griff was still keeping watch around them, but that caused him to turn toward the front. Rachel looked, too, and she saw the SUV door open on the driver's side. However, she didn't see the person. Whoever it was stayed hunched behind the door. At first, anyway. But then he staggered out into the open.

Oh, mercy.

It was Buddy.

"Does he have a gun?" Rachel blurted out.

Neither Griff nor Thea answered. And it probably didn't matter, anyway. Because that's when Rachel saw the blood all over the front of Buddy's shirt. He clutched his hand to his chest, his gaze connecting with theirs.

Before he collapsed.

"ARE YOU OKAY?" Griff asked Rachel. He figured she was tired of that question. Griff certainly was. But so far, he hadn't been able to do the necessary things to keep her from nearly being killed.

"I'm okay," Rachel lied.

She glanced at him and then at the road, when the San Antonio cop took the turn toward the ranch. Thankfully, they hadn't had to wait for someone in McCall Canyon to show up and drive them back. No way had Griff wanted to wait around near the hospital with the gunmen possibly still in the area.

"I'm worried about Thea, though," Rachel added.

Yeah, so was he. Unlike Rachel and him, Thea had been taken to the hospital for a possible cracked rib that she'd gotten in the collision. Soon, he'd need to call and check on her, though Egan had assured Griff that he would make sure Thea got back to the ranch safely once the doctor had given her the all clear.

Buddy might not get an all clear, though. He was alive. For now. But Griff wasn't holding out hope that the man would make it. Still, if Buddy could just regain consciousness long enough to tell them who was behind this, then Griff could arrest the person and stop another attack.

That might get that stark, troubled look off Rachel's face.

Of course, they would have to wait awhile to see if Buddy could give them that information. The man was currently in surgery to remove the bullets from his chest, and even if he made it through that, it might be hours before Egan or someone else could get in there to talk to him.

One thing was for certain—Griff wouldn't be doing the interrogation. For that to happen, he'd have to take Rachel away from the ranch again, and he wasn't going to do that.

The San Antonio officer, Detective Wade Martinez, pulled to a stop in front of the ranch house. The door opened, and both Warren and Ruby looked out at them as they hurried in. Martinez waited until they were inside before he drove away.

"We heard what happened," Warren immediately said, checking Rachel as much as she would let him. She gave Ruby a hug and started for the stairs, no doubt so she could go to bed, but stopped when she saw the bag on the table in the foyer.

"It's from Dr. Baldwin," Ruby said. "Lucy Martin's boy, Dave, who's a medic, brought it by for you. He said he was supposed to draw blood, too, but he said he could come back. All you have to do is call him."

Rachel eyed the bag as if she was hesitant about touching it. No doubt because it contained the pregnancy test. After everything that had just happened, she probably wasn't feeling steady enough to do the test, no matter what the results.

"I'll call Dave after I've rested a bit." She took the bag and went up the stairs toward her room.

Griff considered following her, but decided to give her some time. He doubted that she'd be doing much resting, though.

"You need me to fix you a drink?" Ruby asked Griff.

It was tempting, but he didn't need alcohol clouding his head. The fatigue and spent adrenaline were already doing enough of that. He thanked her, though, and Ruby excused herself to go to the kitchen.

"Does Rachel blame me for this?" Warren asked.

Because of his fuzzy head it took Griff a moment to realize what Warren meant. "You mean because Buddy was your CI?" He didn't wait for Warren to confirm that. "No. She doesn't blame you. You had no way of knowing that Buddy would do something like this."

Warren shook his head. "I'm the one who invited him into my life."

"Nearly everyone who's been in law enforcement has dealt with a CI," Griff argued. "Plus Buddy could have been just a patsy. He could have been lured to this crime scene the way someone lured you to Silver Creek."

Warren stared at him, nodded and then patted his arm. "Thanks."

"For what? Believing you?"

"For believing *in* me. But then, you always have."

That seemed like some kind of apology for something. Maybe because Warren had always thought Griff wasn't good enough for Rachel. But there was no apology needed. If their situations had been reversed, Griff might have felt the same way.

"Go ahead," Warren prompted. "Make sure Rachel's okay." He gave him a pat on the back and walked away.

Griff went up the stairs, but he didn't intend to see Rachel. Instead, he was going to the guest room that was next to hers. Or at least that was the plan. But it got derailed when he found her door open, and saw her standing in the doorway of her bathroom, holding one of the pregnancy test sticks in her hand.

She looked up and their gazes connected. "The package said to wait three minutes. It'll be a plus sign if it's positive and a minus sign if it's negative."

All right. Griff wasn't sure if those three minutes were up or not, because Rachel didn't add anything else. She went to the foot of her bed and sat down. No way did he want her to be alone for this, so Griff went in, shutting the door behind him. He walked over and eased down next to her, but she was holding her thumb over the little screen on the test.

"It's terrifying," she added. "And exciting." She had that same apologetic look in her eyes as Warren had earlier.

"It's the same for me," Griff admitted, though right now the terror was winning out.

Since Rachel looked as if she could use it, he brushed a kiss on her cheek. What he hadn't expected her to do was lean against him. She dropped her head onto his shoulder.

"I thought maybe you'd want to punch me or something right about now," Griff said.

Rachel lifted her head, met his gaze. "You mean because of the attack or the possible pregnancy?"

"Either. Both."

Now she brushed a kiss on his cheek. "We've both been through the wringer. I think it's best if we declare a truce."

Considering that just hours ago he'd kissed her, it felt as if they were well past the truce stage.

Well past three minutes, too, for the test.

Griff was about to move her thumb so they could see the results, but his phone rang before he could do that. When he saw Egan's name on the screen, he knew it was a call he had to take.

"Is Thea okay?" Griff asked the moment he answered. He put the call on speaker so that Rachel could hear.

"She's fine. No cracked or broken ribs. Just a deep bruise. Egan said Ian will take her to the ranch so she can spend the night there, but I'll need him back here once he's dropped her off."

Yes, probably because Egan was neck-deep in this investigation. Griff would help with it in any way he could, but his top priority was keeping Rachel safe.

"Buddy didn't make it through surgery," Egan added a moment later. "And he didn't say anything to the medical staff."

Griff tried not to feel the punch of dread that came along with that, since he'd been expecting it. Still, it stung. Apparently it did for Rachel, too, because she groaned softly.

"What about the San Antonio PD?" Griff asked. "Do they have anything on the shooter who killed Buddy?"

"Not so far, but there were several traffic cameras in the area. They'll access the footage and go from there. This is their jurisdiction, but they'll keep us in the loop since the attack's probably tied to the ones on Rachel and you."

The chances were indeed high that it was tied to them, but Buddy was a CI, which meant he could have had someone who wanted him dead. There was some support for that theory, as well, since the shooter hadn't attempted to gun down Rachel and him. Of course, the killer could have made Buddy a priority if the man had intended to rat out the person who'd hired him.

"I'll bring in Marlon again to see if he knows anything about Buddy," Egan added. "Who knows, he might surprise me and tell me the truth."

That would indeed be a surprise, but there was another possible player in this, too. "What about Brad?"

Egan's heavy sigh let Griff know that getting the DA in was a little trickier than questioning Marlon. "I'll see what I can do."

"If you think he's innocent—" Griff started to say, but Egan interrupted him.

"I don't. I mean, I don't know if he's innocent or not. I don't like the way he keeps pushing Rachel. It's obvious he's jealous of you and her. I just don't know if he'd be willing to take jealousy as far as murder."

That was the big question, and maybe Egan would be able to get the answer. Answers about Alma and Simon, too, since they were still on the suspect list.

"How's Rachel?" Egan asked.

Griff looked at her, but didn't have a clue about that. "I'm just tired," she answered. "Let us know if you get anything from Marlon or Brad."

Egan assured her that he would, and ended the call. Rachel didn't move. She just sat there, her attention now on the pregnancy test. She pulled back her thumb, and that's when Griff saw it.

The plus sign.

Rachel was pregnant.

Chapter Thirteen

Rachel forced herself out of the shower. She'd already been in there way too long, and it wasn't helping her relax as it usually did. But then, there was probably nothing that would take away the tension she was feeling.

Griff likely wasn't faring much better. After she'd seen that plus sign on the pregnancy test, Rachel had practically kicked him out of her bedroom, using the excuse that she needed to rest. She had. She was exhausted. But after two hours of trying to take a nap, she'd finally given up on it and tried the shower. Since this hadn't worked, she would just have to face the problem head-on and go and talk to Griff.

The problem was she didn't know what to say.

Yes, Griff had been nothing but supportive and would continue to be, but never once had she heard him talk about having children. And now that was being forced on him.

Rachel certainly didn't feel that way. With each

passing minute her mind was moving from the problems this pregnancy would create to the fact that in about eight months she would be a mother. A thought that no longer terrified her. In fact, she was starting to imagine herself holding her baby. Raising it. Loving it.

So maybe the shower had helped, after all.

She dried off and got dressed, since she would need to go downstairs and make an appearance. It was 9:00 p.m., but Griff, Ruby, Thea and her father would no doubt be waiting to see if she was okay. She'd have to put on a front for them so they wouldn't worry more than they already were.

Rachel glanced at her phone and groaned when she saw the missed call from Egan. Since it could be important, she called him back right away, and he immediately picked up.

"What's wrong?" she asked.

Egan didn't jump to say anything, which probably wasn't a good sign. "I got worried when you didn't answer."

"Sorry. I was in the shower. Did something happen?" And she tried to prepare herself for the worst. "Is Mom okay?"

"Mom's fine, but Marlon's missing. I already let Griff know this, but I called Marlon to come in for questioning, and when he didn't answer, I had a Silver Creek deputy go check on him. His folks said he packed a bag, took the spare cash they keep in the inn's safe and left."

That didn't sound like something an innocent man would do. "Can you put out an APB on him?"

"Already done that. If and when he turns up, I'll let you know. I've also told the hands to be on the lookout in case he goes to the ranch."

That caused her chest to feel tight. No way did she want Marlon anywhere near here. "What about Alma and Simon? Will you be questioning them again, too?"

"Oh, yeah. First thing in the morning. Alma's at home. Raleigh called to tell me that. I don't know about Simon. Like Marlon, he didn't answer, but there's no sign he's on the run or anything."

No, but that didn't mean he wasn't responsible for what was going on. Rachel had ruled out Alma as being behind this, but she certainly hadn't ruled out Simon.

And that left her with one other suspect she wanted to ask about. "Any idea where Brad is?"

"Not missing, that's for sure. He just stormed out of here." Egan paused. "I'm beginning to think Brad has spies everywhere."

Rachel made a sound of agreement. "He said he's got someone keeping an eye on Mom."

"Yeah, I'm fixing that. It's a nurse, and I got her name from Brad." He paused again. "I also got something else from Brad. He said you had a pregnancy test delivered to the ranch. Is it true?"

She could have sworn her heart skipped a beat. "How did Brad know that?"

Egan groaned. "So it's true. And as for how he knows, my guess is he's got a spy or two here in town, as well. Are you pregnant?" He came right out and asked the question.

Rachel considered dodging it, but her brother wasn't a fool, so he probably already knew the answer. "I don't have test results yet, but I'm sure I am."

He didn't groan again, but Rachel could practically feel him scowling. "It's Griff's baby," he stated. "And no, you don't have to confirm it. Griff didn't, by the way, when I asked him about it."

"You what?" she snapped. "Why would you ask Griff something like that?"

"Because I told him that Brad knew about a pregnancy test being delivered to you at the ranch, and I figured Griff's several moments of stunned silence said everything I needed to know. Do you need me to kick his butt for you?"

It was such a big-brother thing to say. "No." But she apparently did need to talk to Griff. He was probably beating himself up right about now. "Just keep this to yourself," she added. "Because I don't want it getting back to Mom until I've had a chance to tell her."

She ended the call with Egan and went out into the hall. She could hear her father and Ruby chatting about some food deliveries they needed to postpone because of security reasons. Since Griff didn't seem to be in on that conversation, she went to his room, and when she knocked, it was only a few seconds before the door flew open.

And she saw Griff naked.

Well, almost naked, anyway. He wasn't wearing a shirt, and even though he was wearing jeans, they weren't zipped all the way. Judging from his damp hair and soap scent, he'd just gotten out of the shower. Rachel hoped it'd done him more good than it had her, but his expression said otherwise.

He still had a towel in his hand, but he stepped back so she could come inside. "You talked to Egan," he said, shutting the door.

She nodded. "He knows I'm pregnant."

Griff's eyebrows lifted. "Is he on his way over here to beat me to a pulp?"

Rachel couldn't help it; she smiled. Though this definitely wasn't a smiling situation. "Egan will accept this." Only because he didn't have another choice. "He just wants to make sure I'm okay."

Griff stared at her. "Are you?"

She stared back. Which probably wasn't a good idea because of his lack of clothes. She had some incredible memories of touching and kissing his bare chest, and seeing him like this brought all that back. Not just the memories but also the heat that went along with them.

"Are *you* okay?" she asked, turning the tables on him.

He gave one of those half smiles, put the towel aside and reached for his shirt, which he'd draped over the back of a chair. Part of her hated that he was covering up, but Griff must have known it wasn't a good idea for them to be behind closed doors while one of them was half-naked.

He walked closer to her while he was still buttoning his shirt, and she took in more of his scent. The soap, yes, but Griff's own scent was beneath that, and it gave her body another of those heated tugs that she didn't need.

"Since Brad knows about the pregnancy test," Griff said, "I'm sure he can guess what went on between us."

That didn't erase the heat she was feeling for Griff, but it did cool her down some. That's because she followed it to an easy-to-see conclusion. Brad was already upset with her, and this definitely wouldn't help. But would he do something stupid?

Maybe use his spies to spill the news to her mother?

"Yeah," Griff mumbled, when she groaned. "You definitely need to keep your distance from him. And

Court will make sure Brad doesn't have any contact with your mom."

"That's a good start. But I should tell my mother."

"After what happened earlier, you're not going to the hospital." He sounded like a lawman with that order.

"No," she agreed. She could still hear the sound of those gunshots. "I can call her in the morning."

Though she hated to give her mom that kind of news over the phone. At least she'd be able to tell her father and Ruby in person, and Rachel turned to go downstairs to do that. But that meant walking past Griff.

He was clothed now. For the most part, anyway. His jeans were still unzipped, and he'd missed the bottom buttons on his shirt. The opening created enough of a gap for her to see some of his stomach. And just like that, more memories came. She hadn't been sure anything could stop the sounds of the attack in her head, but she'd been wrong. That stopped it.

Worse, Griff had followed her gaze and knew what had caught her attention.

Their eyes met, connected, and he seemed to be waiting for her to do something. Maybe for her to make the first move. Or to come to her senses and leave. He had no doubt figured that he shouldn't be the one to start something that shouldn't happen in the first place.

At least that's what she thought.

But she was wrong.

Griff cursed, the profanity aimed at himself, and he reached out, sliding his hand around the back of her neck. Still cursing, he pulled her to him and kissed her.

FROM THE MOMENT that Rachel had come into his room, Griff had told himself to keep his distance from her. That hadn't worked right from the start, because he'd seen the heated look in her eyes.

A look that he was certain was in his own eyes, too.

But with some willpower, he could have kept it at just a look. Apparently, though, he was fresh out of any shred of willpower tonight.

The kiss sure didn't help, either. Because there was plenty of fire when he touched his mouth to hers.

Still, he could have forced himself to back away *if* Rachel hadn't made that silky sound of pleasure. Along with that, she moved her body right against his. Griff knew that no amount of willpower was going to stand a chance about that.

It was Rachel who deepened the kiss, and she slipped right into his arms as if she belonged there. Certain parts of his body believed that she *did* belong there. But Griff tried to hang on to what little common sense he had left.

"You're pregnant," he reminded her, though it apparently was a dumb thing to do.

She pulled back, blinked, and even though she didn't come out and voice it, her expression said, *"So?"*

She was right, of course. Pregnant women kissed and had sex. Still, most women probably didn't do that when they were still coming to terms with their condition.

"This could be a reaction to the spent adrenaline," he murmured, trying again.

It wasn't any stronger an argument than the pregnancy one—even if it was a possibility. Obviously, though, Rachel wasn't going to let that get in the way, because she came right back to him for another kiss.

The first kiss was tame compared to this one. This was foreplay, plain and simple. And Griff knew if he was going to put a stop to this, then it had to be now. His mistake was savoring the kiss and the feel of her a little bit longer. It was just enough time for him to pass the point of no return.

Cursing himself again, he hooked his arm around her waist, snapped her to him and did his own share of deepening the kiss. Once he'd done that, he knew this would lead to only one place.

The bed.

Thankfully, they weren't that far away from it. Judging from the sudden urgency of Rachel's kisses, the foreplay wasn't going to last that long. It hadn't the other time they'd been together, either, but he intended to savor this no matter how soon it ended.

Rachel slid her hand in the opening of his shirt, her palm landing on his stomach. And she touched him. Along with that kiss, it packed a punch, and the punch got stronger when she pulled him against her so that their bodies were aligned in a perfect way. Well, it would have been perfect if she hadn't had on so many clothes.

Griff did something about that.

Rachel was wearing a loose cotton dress, and he caught the bottom of it, pulling it off over her head. Of course, that meant breaking the kiss for a couple seconds, but they went right back to it as soon as he tossed the dress aside.

He wasn't the only one with the notion of getting naked, because Rachel rid him of his shirt. Or rather, she did after torturing him while she unfastened the rest of his buttons. The process involved a lot of touching, and by the time she'd gotten it off him, Griff was burning for her.

The burn went up a huge notch when he unclipped her bra and her breasts spilled out into his hands. No way could he miss not kissing her there, so he lowered his head, took her nipple into his mouth and got rewarded with another of those silky sounds of pleasure.

Even though she was clearly enjoying it, Rachel

didn't let the breast kisses go on much longer. She went after his jeans, unzipping him, and slid her hand down into his boxers. That did it for foreplay, and Griff hoisted her up and carried her to the bed.

He kept kissing her when he put her on the mattress, but hadn't planned on landing on top of her. He'd intended to drop down by her side. Rachel, however, pulled him down so they were face-to-face. There weren't many things that could have gotten Griff to slow down, but seeing her did it.

Man, she was beautiful.

She always had been, but she seemed even more so now. Maybe because of the fire that was in her eyes. Or maybe because of the way she was looking at him. Griff reminded himself that this was about lust, but at the moment it seemed like a whole lot more.

She held the eye contact while she shoved off his boxers. Griff did the same when he rid her of her panties. He wanted to hold on to this for a long time, but that wasn't possible. Rachel lifted her hips, taking him inside her, and Griff knew it would be over much too soon.

Because his body gave him no choice, he moved, pushing into all that tight heat. And Rachel moved, too. There was definitely no hesitation as she took everything he was giving her and gave just as much right back.

Soon, very soon, Griff's mind went to a place

where reason didn't exist. He had to finish this. Had to finish her so they could find some kind of release.

He adjusted her enough to give her the pressure she needed. It didn't matter that they had been together only one other time. Griff just seemed to know the rhythm of her body. And he carried her right over the edge.

Rachel made another sound. It was more of that silky pleasure mixed with relief. That was his cue to let himself go. Griff gathered her into his arms, kissed her and gave in to the fire.

Chapter Fourteen

Griff's kiss felt a little bittersweet to Rachel. She'd known that the sex wouldn't last, but the kiss—and his climax—were a reminder that it might be a while before this could happen again.

If ever.

Now that some of the fire had been sated, Griff might remember that this was the last thing they should be doing. After all, there was a would-be killer still out there somewhere, and Griff, she and her entire family were in danger. His sister, too, since she was in the house. Sex shouldn't have been on the agenda, and yet it'd seemed as necessary to Rachel as taking her next breath.

When Griff lifted his head, she saw the regret that was already starting to show in his eyes. Rachel huffed and kissed him again. He tasted just as good as he looked, and at first she thought she could keep him in the moment if the kisses continued. But

Griff grumbled something and rolled off her, landing on his back.

"The baby," he said. "I don't want to hurt you."

Oh.

Rachel certainly hadn't forgotten about being pregnant, but she'd become so lost in the pleasure that she hadn't considered it might not be a good idea for Griff's weight to be on her like that. Still, she hated the fact that he was no longer inside her.

Griff helped, though, with that loss she felt. He pulled her into the crook of his arm so that their bodies were touching. It wasn't anywhere near as intimate as sex, but it was still nice. Plus she had a great view of his naked body. There was something to be said for that.

"I'm not going to say I'm sorry for this," he told her.

Good. That was a start. Rachel had been afraid he was going to put all the blame for this on his shoulders. If there was any blame, that is.

"There's no reason for you to apologize. I started it," she reminded him. "I kissed you first."

She considered adding more to that, but it probably wasn't a smart idea to admit to Griff that she'd been thinking about getting him naked. Not just tonight, either. She'd been thinking about it for weeks.

Heck, for years.

He leaned over, kissed her. "This should make us even then." And he let the kiss linger for a few steamy moments.

No, it only made her want him all over again, but when Griff sat up, she figured that wasn't going to happen. "I need to check on Thea," he stated.

"Thea?" Rachel hadn't expected him to bring up his sister at a time like this. "Is she okay?"

"She's fine. When I checked on her about an hour ago, she was keeping watch over the backyard," Griff explained while he put on his shoulder holster. "I just need to make sure she doesn't need a break, because she probably won't ask for one. And then I need to see if the San Antonio PD found anything on those traffic cameras on the street where Buddy was murdered. Plus you need to eat something, so you should come downstairs with me."

She wasn't the least bit hungry, but when he glanced at her stomach, she realized he was probably concerned about the baby. Or so she thought. But then he ducked his head, his mouth lingering a moment over her abdomen. He waited until he had eye contact with her before he planted a scorching kiss just below her navel.

It was a nice moment, but it didn't last, of course. He groaned again, got up and started dressing. Rachel watched for a moment, just enjoying the view, but then got up, as well. She'd barely managed to put on her clothes when her phone rang, and when she fished it out of her pocket, she saw her mother's name on the screen.

Her heart dropped.

It was past regular visiting hours, which meant it was too late for her mother to be making a routine call. So Rachel immediately answered.

"Mom, are you okay?" she blurted out.

That got Griff's attention, and he hurried to her. Rachel put the call on speaker so he could hear.

"People have been keeping things from me so that it won't upset me. I don't like that," her mother said.

That certainly didn't sound like the threat Rachel had thought she might hear her say. "What kind of things?" And while she had her on the phone, Rachel tacked on another question. "And why did want to see Alma Lawton?"

"I, uh, just wanted to meet Alma face-to-face, to ask her…why she'd had an affair and a son with my husband. I needed to know why Warren was with her and if he loved her."

Rachel sighed. "Mom, I understand why you'd want to talk to her about that, but I'm not sure knowing will help."

Great. She heard her mother start to sob, and more than anything Rachel wanted to be there with her. To assure her that things were going to get better. At least she hoped they would.

"Are you in love with Griff?" Helen asked.

Rachel was certain that put a shocked look on her face, and it did the same to Griff. "Who told you that?" she pressed. "Was it Brad?"

"Brad? No, I haven't seen or heard from him in a while now. No, this came from that other man who called me. He said his name was Marlon Stowe."

Everything inside Rachel went still. "When did you talk to Marlon?"

"I just got off the phone with him."

"I'll make sure Marlon's not at the hospital," Griff said, taking out his phone. He moved away from her to make the call.

"Mom, what else did Marlon say?" Rachel continued.

"That you've been staying at the ranch with Griff. That you've been sleeping with him."

Rachel couldn't deny any of that, but she wondered if it was a guess on Marlon's part or if he had the ranch under surveillance. If he was watching them with infrared binoculars, Marlon might be able to tell that she'd been with Griff in his guest room. The thought of him spying on them turned her stomach.

"Marlon was upset with you," her mother went on, "because he said you lied to his girlfriend and that now she's very angry with him. I told him you weren't a liar, but he insisted that you were, that you'd ruined his life. He wanted me to talk to you, to convince you to go to his girlfriend and tell her that you'd made a mistake."

Hearing each word caused Rachel's muscles to tighten. "I didn't make a mistake. Marlon isn't a nice man, and if he ever calls you again or tries to visit you, you're to let the staff know immediately."

Her mother sobbed again. "You're scaring me, Rachel."

"I'm sorry. I don't want to say these things to you, but it's important that you understand."

"I do understand. But please don't tell my doctor that Marlon's call upset me. He might take my phone away."

That might not be such a bad idea. But Rachel didn't want to do that just yet since it might make her mother feel even worse not to be able to call her kids whenever she wanted. However, Rachel did need to have a conversation with the staff about at least monitoring the incoming calls. Especially calls from Marlon, Alma or Simon.

"You didn't answer my question about you being in love with Griff," her mother said several moments later.

No, she hadn't answered, and Rachel didn't intend to do that. Not in front of Griff, anyway. Her feelings for him were, well, complicated, and she needed to work them out for herself before she started sharing that with others.

Besides, Rachel doubted Griff wanted to hear the *l* word from her since he no doubt was having to deal with his own feelings. Not just about the pregnancy and her but also the threats to their lives. Those threats were much worse and the stakes much higher now that there was a baby involved.

Rachel told her mother good-night and then looked up at Griff. He was by the door, but maybe he was waiting to see if she was going to bring up any part of the conversation she'd just had. She wasn't.

"Why don't you go ahead and check on Thea," she settled for saying.

Griff opened his mouth, then closed it as if he'd changed his mind about what to say. "Come with me and get something to eat."

Since she should have at least a snack, Rachel got up to follow him. However, they'd made it only a few steps before there was a slight crackling sound.

And the room was suddenly plunged into darkness.

GRIFF AUTOMATICALLY PUT his hand over his gun.

He assured himself that this could be nothing, but after everything else that had been going on for the past two days, he didn't want to take a chance.

"The generator should kick in soon," Rachel said. "It won't be full power, but at least we'll have the security system and the lights."

The security system was a must. No way did he want someone breaking in without them knowing.

Griff waited for the generator. And waited. But nothing happened. It was too much to hope that it was simply malfunctioning.

He went to the window and looked out. There were no signs of an intruder. No signs of ranch hands, either, but the last time he'd checked on them, two were on the front porch. With Thea keeping watch at the back of the house, the three should have been able to see anyone approaching from the sides or the road.

"Are the lights out in Court's place, too?" Rachel asked.

Griff looked in that direction, but didn't see anything. That could be because Court had turned off the lights when he went to the hospital to be with his mother. And Court's fiancée, Rayna, wasn't there because last Griff had heard, Court had her staying with friends in a nearby town, instead of coming back to McCall Canyon after the horse show. With Buddy's killer still on the loose, Court hadn't wanted her there alone, and Rayna hadn't wanted to stay at the main house.

"You think something's wrong," Rachel said. Her voice was a little shaky, probably because she already knew the answer to that question.

Yeah, he thought something was wrong, but Griff hoped this was all just a bad coincidence.

"Don't go near the window just in case," he warned her, and he went to the door. He didn't open it yet, but instead put his ear to it and listened for any unusual sounds.

Nothing.

And there should have been *something*. By now, Warren or Thea should have been checking on them to make sure they were all right. But the house was quiet. Too quiet.

"Call your father or Ruby to make sure they're okay," Griff instructed.

Behind him, he could hear Rachel taking out her phone. A moment later, he also heard the curse word that she mumbled under her breath. "My screen says there's no service."

Griff took out his own phone and saw the same thing.

Hell.

There were dead zones for cell reception all over the ranch, but Griff had made at least a dozen calls from this room without any problem. And since the electricity being off wouldn't have affected the service, then it likely meant someone had managed to jam the signal. To do that, the person would have had to be darn close to the house.

"Is the security system on battery backup?" Griff asked.

"I'm not sure."

Since the house belonged to a former sheriff, it probably was on backup. If so, that meant the alarm would still go off if they had an intruder.

"Stay back," he warned Rachel as he reached for the doorknob.

He heard her slight gasp and knew she was afraid, but he didn't want to go to her just yet. Not until he'd made sure that everything was okay.

Griff opened the door just a fraction and peered out. Nothing. Well, nothing considering that the hall was even darker than the guest room. Just in case someone was hiding in the shadows, he used the flashlight on his phone to look around, but he still didn't see anything.

Didn't hear anything, either.

"Warren?" he called out.

"I'm here in the foyer," the older man answered.

Relief swept through him. Through Rachel, too, because she released the breath she'd been holding. "Are you okay?" Griff asked.

"Fine. But my phone's messed up. The security system, too, because the lights are all flashing on the monitor by the door."

That definitely wasn't a good sign. "Have you seen anyone?" By anyone, Griff meant an intruder.

"No. But I was about to go to the kitchen to check on Thea. Ruby's in her room, so I'd better make sure she's okay."

Ruby's room was at the end of the hall, and the door was closed. It was possible that the woman had already gone to bed and was asleep. That would explain why she hadn't come out into the hall when the power went off. Still, Griff needed to make sure all was well.

"Let me know if Thea's all right," Griff told Warren, and he glanced back at Rachel. "Wait right here."

Even with just the light from his cell phone, he could see that she looked shaken up. He hated leaving her alone, so Griff took out his backup weapon and handed it to her. That didn't do much to ease the fear in her eyes, but she took the gun, holding it in a death grip.

"Hurry," she said. "And be careful."

He would do both, and because he thought they both needed it, Griff went back and gave her a quick kiss before he stepped out into the hall.

Ruby's room was only four doors down, probably about twenty yards, but it suddenly felt as if it were miles away. Griff made his way along the hall, keeping watch over his shoulder. He thought he might be able to hear someone walking up the stairs, but he didn't want to take any chances, since an intruder coming up that way would get to Rachel before him.

There was a large floor-to-ceiling window at the end of the hall right next to Ruby's room, and Griff had a quick glance outside. And he saw something he darn sure didn't want to see.

Thea.

She was in the backyard and had her gun drawn. Her gaze was darting all around her, the kind of looks a lawman would make who'd heard or spotted something. Definitely not good, because he didn't want his sister or anyone else out there without backup.

There was also another problem.

Thea wouldn't have deliberately disarmed the security system when she went outside, so that confirmed that it wasn't working. Not a good time for that. Now, he only hoped the would-be killer didn't sneak into the back of the house while Thea was outside.

Griff considered opening the window and calling out to his sister, but decided he should go to her instead. So that she'd have backup. That meant first checking on Ruby and then having Warren stay with Rachel.

"Ruby?" Griff knocked on her door, and when she didn't immediately answer, he tried the knob.

Unlocked. But when he opened the door, he saw no signs of the woman. She could be in the bathroom, but going in there meant he wouldn't have line of sight of the guest room, and he didn't want to risk someone getting to Rachel. Or her taking it upon herself to come out into the hall to try to help him.

Griff heard a sound. Not coming from the guest room. This seemed to have come from the foyer. It wasn't footsteps but more like a heavy thud. As if someone had run into something or fallen.

Rachel must have heard it, too, because she hurried to the doorway of the guest room. That sent Griff hurrying to her. Because if there was an intruder in the house, whoever it was might rush up the stairs and try to shoot her.

"You need to stay back," Griff insisted when he reached her, positioning himself at the door.

She shook her head. "But I think something happened to my father."

So did Griff, but he didn't want that *something* to happen to her, as well.

"Warren?" he called out again.

Griff didn't shout because he didn't want his voice to mask the sound of footsteps. But he didn't hear anything. He especially didn't hear Warren's assurance that he was okay.

He didn't get that.

But he did hear something else.

It hadn't come from the foyer, but rather from outside in the backyard.

"Watch out!" someone shouted.

Thea.

And it was followed by another sound that Griff definitely didn't want to hear. His sister screamed.

Chapter Fifteen

Rachel's breath froze. Oh, God. What was happening?

Despite Griff's warning for her to stay away from the guest room window, she ran there, hoping to get a glimpse of Thea. It would give her partial views of the back and side yards. But his sister wasn't visible. No one was.

Griff looked, too, though he volleyed glances between the window and the guest room doorway. Rachel knew the last thing Griff wanted was to take her down those stairs. But that scream changed everything.

"We have to check on her," Rachel insisted.

Griff seemed to have a debate with himself. One that didn't last but a few seconds and ended with him cursing. "I might be able to see Thea from the window at the end of the hall. Stay right next to me."

The moment she nodded, Griff got them moving. He didn't run, exactly, but it was close to that pace as he hurried out of the guest room. He also kept firing glances over his shoulder. And she knew why. If someone had attacked Thea, then he or she could be coming after Griff and her.

But there was another problem.

The scream hadn't been the only thing Rachel had heard. Just moments before that there'd been another sound near the front door. She prayed that no one had managed to break in, because if so that meant the intruder had gotten past the two hands who were on the front porch. She hadn't heard the sound of gunshots, but that didn't mean the men hadn't been harmed in some way.

When they made it to the large hall window, Griff moved her so that her back was against the wall and their sides were to the stairs. He glanced out. So did Rachel. But there was still no sign of Thea.

"My sister was there just a few minutes ago," he mumbled. He tipped his head toward the center of the backyard.

There were no hiding places in that spot, but there was a detached garage about twenty feet away. It was possible Thea had seen something that spooked her and had run there.

"She's a cop," Rachel reminded Griff. "She knows how to take care of herself." And she prayed that Thea had done whatever was necessary to be safe.

Even though they were a good distance from the stairs now, Rachel heard something that she thought was coming from the foyer. It sounded as if someone was moaning in pain. Griff must have thought so, too, because they started moving again—this time with him in front of her.

"Keep watch on the bedrooms in case someone comes out of one," he whispered.

That definitely caused her heartbeat to rev up even more. She hadn't considered that they could be ambushed, but she did now.

If someone was indeed on the second floor of the house, it meant the person had maybe broken in without anyone seeing him or her. Possibly while Griff and she had been making love. No way would she have heard something, and that was the very reason she should have never gone to his bed. In hindsight, that could have been a fatal mistake.

Griff slowed the pace considerably as they started down the stairs. The staircase was curved, and that wasn't an advantage right now because it meant they couldn't see into the foyer until they were halfway down. That's probably why Griff kept pausing and lifting his head. He was listening for any indication that an attacker was nearby.

Each step seemed to take hours, and with each one, her pulse drummed in her ears. The fear came, too, washing over her and making her unsteady. Rachel forced herself to take several long breaths. It didn't help much, but the only thing that would help right now was for her to discover everyone was safe and that this had been a false alarm.

Griff didn't call out to her father or Thea as he crept down the steps. Rachel followed, dismayed when she learned the foyer was pitch-dark. Not good; they couldn't tell if anyone was there or not.

There was another of those moaning sounds, and this time she was able to pinpoint it. It was coming from the family room just off the foyer.

"Make sure no one comes at us from behind." Griff whispered that reminder, and they continued down the steps.

Again her heart started to race, but Rachel kept up, staying close to Griff but also keeping watch. Not just behind but all around them.

When they reached the foyer, Griff went to the front door and tested the knob. It was still locked. But he mumbled some profanity when he looked out the side window to the porch.

"The ranch hands aren't there," he said.

It felt as if her stomach went to her knees. There was no way the men would voluntarily leave their posts. Not when they knew that a killer was after Griff and her. And that meant someone had either lured them away...

Or killed them.

She didn't want to ask if there was any blood on the porch, but prayed there wasn't. Enough people had already been hurt or killed because of her, and she didn't want to add the ranch hands to the growing list.

The sound of another moan grabbed her attention, and Rachel frantically looked around until she finally spotted someone on the floor.

"Don't," Griff said, when she started to run in that direction.

She knew he was right, that this could be some kind of trap, but everything inside her was screaming for her to get to the person to make sure he or she was all right. "It could be Thea," she reminded him.

Of course, she hadn't needed to tell him that, and thankfully, Griff didn't act out of emotion. He took slow, cautious steps toward the prone figure while he continued to keep watch. Rachel did the same, and she was holding herself together until she saw who it was.

Her father.

He lay in a crumpled heap on the floor. Just like that all the anger she had for him vanished, and Rachel knew she would do anything to save him.

"Check and see if he's hurt," Griff instructed.

While Rachel went to Warren, Griff's gaze slashed from one area of the house to another. Rachel stooped down, putting her fingers to her father's neck. "He's got a pulse."

Thank God. But she didn't have time to savor the relief, because he moaned again, and his eyes fluttered open for a few seconds. He was barely conscious and obviously in pain, or something, but she couldn't see any blood or any sign of an injury. At least she didn't until she held the light from her phone to his neck, and saw the puncture wound there.

"I think someone drugged him," she managed to say. At least she hoped it was just a drug like the one he'd been given the night before last, and not something lethal.

Griff pivoted toward the other side of the family room, taking aim. Rachel hadn't heard anything in that direction, but soon saw someone.

Ruby.

The woman was cowering in the corner next to an armchair. "Warren told me to run and hide," she said. Her voice was shaking so much it was hard to understand her.

With Griff still standing guard, Rachel hurried to her, and as she'd done with her father, she checked Ruby to make sure she hadn't been hurt. There were no signs of injury, and unlike Warren, it didn't seem as if she'd been drugged.

"A man's in the house," Ruby said, her words rushing out with her breath.

Rachel's breath did some rushing, too. Oh, God. Someone *had* broken in.

She looked around. So did Griff. But Rachel didn't see anyone. Whoever it was, though, had probably drugged her father. He was also likely responsible for the missing ranch hands.

And for Thea's scream.

But what Rachel still didn't know—was the intruder one of their suspects? Was it Marlon, Simon or Brad? Or maybe it was just a hired gun who'd been sent there to kill them.

"Did you recognize the man?" Rachel asked in a low voice.

Ruby shook her head. "He was wearing a mask so I didn't get a look at his face. Warren told me to hide," the woman repeated.

That was a good thing or else Ruby would have ended up on that floor. Or she could have ended up dead if she'd fought back.

Griff glanced around again, and Rachel could tell he was trying to figure out what to do. He didn't want to leave them there while he went to find Thea, but he couldn't exactly take them with him, either.

"See if your father's gun is still on him," Griff told Rachel. "If it is, give it to Ruby."

Rachel scrambled back to her dad so she could check, and found the small gun he carried in a boot holster. He'd probably had his primary weapon in his hand when he'd been attacked, which meant the intruder had taken it. Not exactly a comforting thought, though the snake had almost certainly brought his own weapons with him.

But why hadn't he just come in with guns blazing? And why hadn't he killed Warren?

Maybe this was some kind of sick cat-and-mouse game as he tried to get to Griff and her. If so, it could be working. Because they couldn't just stay put, not with Thea in possible danger. Heck, they couldn't even call for backup.

She brought the gun to Ruby, and even though the woman was shaking badly, Rachel knew she could shoot. It came with the territory of working on a ranch, since snakes often came into the yard.

"Keep watch," Griff instructed Rachel, and while she did that, he helped her father to his feet and moved him to the corner with Ruby. It wasn't ideal cover, but it'd been an effective hiding place for her, and at least they weren't out in the open.

Once Griff had finished, he turned back to Rachel. "You can stay here with them while I look for Thea."

She was shaking her head before he even finished. "You need someone to watch your back." Rachel paused and wished there was a better way to put this. There wasn't. "This person is after us. If we're apart, it'll only make it easier for him."

She could tell that Griff wanted to come up with a good argument for her to stay put. But he couldn't. The safest place for her to be was with him, and yet it might not be safe at all.

Griff must have realized there was no time to debate this, so he nodded. Other than their cell phones, there wasn't any other light in the room, but it was enough for her to see his worried expression. Still, he motioned for her to follow him.

"Stay close and watch our backs. I'm sorry it has to be this way," he added. "And if something goes wrong, just get down as fast as you can. Don't try to return fire or fight this guy."

"All right," she agreed, but it wasn't something she could promise. No way would she just stand by if someone was trying to kill Griff.

With her breath stalled in her throat, Rachel followed him out of the family room. As he'd done on the stairs, he kept his footsteps slow while he gazed around him. Rachel watched, too, and listened, but didn't hear anything. She wasn't sure if that was a good sign or not.

They made their way through the dining room. The windows were all shut in there, but when they got to the kitchen, Rachel immediately spotted the open door.

A new jolt of fear came because Griff had said he'd seen Thea in the backyard. If the intruder had gotten into the house this way, he would have gone right past her, and that might have been about the time she'd screamed.

Griff's steps slowed even more as he scanned the kitchen island and the breakfast nook. No one was there. But a passageway to their left led to an eat-in kitchen. It was too dark to see much of anything there. However, Rachel did see something on the other side of the room.

Another partially open door. This one to the pantry.

It wasn't an ideal hiding place, since there was only one entrance. If the intruder was in there, then he was trapped.

Or waiting for them to come closer.

Griff motioned for her to get lower. Rachel did, so did he, and while they crouched down, they started for the pantry. But they'd made it only a few steps when he stopped.

"Use your phone to light up that area on the floor," he whispered, motioning to a spot several feet from the pantry door.

Rachel did. She reached around him, shining the light on the tile, and that's when she saw what had captured his attention. The dark colored drops and spatters. And she had no doubts as to what it was.

Blood.

GRIFF PRAYED THAT the blood belonged to the intruder and not Thea or one of the now missing ranch hands.

Of course, if it wasn't his sister's or that of someone else helping them, it meant Rachel and he were possibly about to have a showdown with the snake who'd orchestrated all this, since the blood drops led right to the pantry. Griff would have welcomed that if Rachel hadn't been right behind him.

He considered taking her back into the family room to wait with Ruby and Warren, but if the intruder was in the pantry and Rachel was truly his target, he'd probably just try to gun them down if they ran. Well, he would try that if he was capable of shooting. Maybe he was too injured to do so.

Better yet, maybe he was dead.

A dead man wouldn't be able to give them answers about the previous attacks, but he wouldn't be able to harm Rachel, either. Griff would give up those answers about why this was happening if it meant keeping her safe. Heck, he'd give up anything to make sure that happened. Because it wasn't just Rachel's life that was at stake now. So was their child's.

Griff dragged in a deep breath and started inching toward the pantry door. He kept his gun ready while he continued to glance around them. After all, the blood and the open pantry door could be a trick so the guy could sneak up on them. When he reached the door, Griff looked inside.

And he came face-to-face with a gun.

"Don't shoot," someone mumbled.

It was Thea. She was sprawled out on the floor, her back against the wall and her gun aimed right at him. Griff also saw the source of the blood. It was coming from the left side of her head.

Griff glanced around the pantry. Like the rest of the house, it was large, with rows of shelves and stacked boxes of supplies. Still, he could take it all in with a sweeping glance, and when he didn't see anyone with Thea, he pulled Rachel inside, then stepped behind her, staying close to the door in case he had to return fire or get them out of there fast.

"A man sneaked up on me and clubbed me," Thea whispered, her words slurred. "I tried to shout a warning to all of you, but he hit me on the head and took my gun. I had a backup weapon on me, though." She rubbed her neck and winced. "He gave me some kind of shot, too, but I don't think I got the full dose. That's because I pushed the needle away and ran."

It was probably a drug to knock her out, as the intruder had done to Warren, and judging from the way she was talking and her unfocused eyes, the drug was working. That wasn't good, but Griff reminded himself that it could have been a lot worse. If Thea's attacker had gotten close enough to hit her, then he could have easily shot and killed her.

So why hadn't he?

The answer to that twisted him up inside. Because this snake wanted Rachel. It had been that way right from the start of the attacks, and unfortunately, it didn't rule out any of their suspects.

"Did you recognize the man who did this to you?" Griff asked his sister.

Thea shook her head and winced again. She was obviously in pain, but Griff had no way to call for an ambulance. He only hoped the injury wasn't serious.

Rachel grabbed some paper napkins from one of the shelves and pressed them to Thea's head, obviously trying to stop the bleeding.

"He's wearing a mask," she explained a moment later. "But whoever it was, he must have come from the front on foot because I didn't hear a car engine. I was watching the back and the sides of the house, so I know he didn't come from anywhere in my direction."

Yes, unless he'd managed to sneak past Thea. But that didn't seem likely. That meant the guy had probably gone after the ranch hands first. But it was darn bold of him to attack two armed men with just a club.

"The back door's open," Rachel said. She was whispering, too. "Did you do that or did your attacker?"

"I don't know. Maybe I left it open when I ran in. Everything's getting fuzzy. I tried to run to the stairs so I could get to Griff and you, but then I got woozy, so I ducked in here. If the guy came in this way, I didn't hear him."

So how had he gotten in? Griff knew for a fact that he was inside because he'd attacked Warren. That meant he was likely hiding somewhere, waiting to strike. Too bad the house was huge, because all the rooms would give this clown lots of places to lie in wait.

"Do you think you can move?" he asked his sister.

Thea nodded and took the paper napkins from Rachel. "But I can't see straight enough to shoot."

"I don't want you for backup." Rachel and he helped Thea to her feet. "I'll leave you both with Warren and Ruby in the family room so I can find this guy."

They looked at him. "You shouldn't do that alone," Rachel whispered.

No, he shouldn't. But he didn't have a lot of options here. He had a cop and former cop, both drugged, which meant it would fall to Rachel and Ruby to protect them.

Definitely not ideal circumstances.

But it wasn't wise to go searching through the house with them in tow while he was looking for a killer. Maybe this guy would just come after him so Griff could put a fast end to it.

He didn't remind Rachel to keep watch—she was already doing that. She also clutched the backup gun he'd given her. With his arm hooked around Thea's waist, he leaned out from the pantry to make sure someone hadn't sneaked into the kitchen. If the intruder had managed to do that, Griff didn't see any signs of him.

Before he moved Thea and Rachel out of the pantry, he went over and shut the outer door. It wouldn't keep someone out, but at least he'd be able to hear if it opened. After all, the intruder who'd entered might not have come alone. He could have hired thugs waiting outside to finish them off if he didn't succeed.

Griff had a quick debate with himself about where to position Rachel, and he finally decided to place her on the other side of Thea. It took him a couple seconds to get them lined up in a way that they'd all be able to use their guns if necessary.

Griff prayed that it wouldn't come down to that.

Because if it did, that meant Rachel and the baby would be in the line of fire.

He moved as fast as he could, which wasn't very fast considering that Thea kept stumbling. Plus he had to keep watch. Not easy as they made their way through the massive house.

They'd just made it back to the dining room when he heard something. Footsteps, maybe. And they weren't coming from the family room just ahead. No, these were coming from behind them.

He pivoted, putting himself in front of Thea and Rachel. Griff brought up his gun. But he didn't see anything so he waited and listened.

Thankfully, he'd been to the McCall home so many times that he knew the layout like the back of his hand. With the kitchen door closed, that meant the person hadn't come in from outside. So, he was probably coming from the direction of the living room. Unfortunately, he could cut through the family room to make it back to the foyer. If that happened, Ruby and Warren could be sitting ducks.

So could Thea, Rachel and Griff.

Because the intruder could come at them from the side. With where they were standing, they'd be easy targets.

"Get all the way down on the floor by the hutch," Griff whispered to Rachel and Thea. It wasn't much cover, but it was the only solid piece of furniture in the room.

Rachel nodded and took hold of Thea to do that. While the movement was necessary, the rustling it made could be masking the sound of other footsteps. Not good. Because Griff needed to be able to pinpoint the location of the goon if he got any closer.

The moment Rachel and Thea quit moving, he heard what he'd been listening for: another footstep. And it seemed to be coming from the foyer. The intruder was probably heading toward them. Griff turned in that direction, but it was already too late.

The shot came right at him.

Chapter Sixteen

Rachel could have sworn the sound of that shot stopped her heart for several seconds. Oh, God. Griff could have been hit.

She frantically looked up, checking for signs of an injury. She didn't see any; thankfully, the bullet had smacked into the wall right next to where Griff was standing.

Rachel reached out, catching his arm and pulling him to the floor. He'd already started to crouch down, and landed right next to Thea and her. However, he didn't stay down. He jumped up, ready to fire, but when he cursed, Rachel guessed the shooter wasn't in sight.

"Keep watch toward the kitchen," Griff whispered to her. "He could circle back around and come at us from that angle."

Rachel hadn't needed anything else to make her more alert, but that did cause her stomach to knot. This stress couldn't be good for the baby.

It also couldn't be good for Thea.

Griff's sister was obviously trying to fight off the effects of whatever drug she'd been given, but she was also in pain. She groaned or winced every time she moved. That didn't make her a good candidate for backing up Griff if she had to return fire. Rachel wasn't exactly a good one, either, because there was no way Griff was going to let her put herself in danger. That meant staying on the floor while he came out from cover to try to put a stop to this.

There was one hope in all of this. Maybe by now Court or Egan had tried calling the ranch, and would have known something was wrong when no one answered. If so, they could be on their way here right now. Maybe they would get to them before someone else got hurt.

Despite her heartbeat crashing in her ears, Rachel forced herself to try to listen for any sounds of the intruder, and she definitely kept her eye on the kitchen area. Unfortunately, there were spots she couldn't see, and if the shooter wanted to sneak up on them, he could duck behind the large kitchen island and make his way closer. If he did that, he'd have a clean shot of Thea and her.

Thea was trembling all over now, but was obviously still trying to fight off the effects of the drug. It was a battle she seemed to be losing, so Rachel moved in front of her, sandwiching her against the wall and the china hutch.

The new position put Rachel at a better angle if she had to shoot into the kitchen. She wasn't an expert shot by any means, but if the intruder showed himself, she would fire at him. Even if she didn't hit him, it might give Griff enough time to adjust his aim and take out the guy.

Rachel heard some movement straight ahead. Someone was on the other side of the wall, which meant he could be going either to the kitchen or back to the family room. She prayed it would be the kitchen, since that would keep this monster away from her father and Ruby.

Because she was so focused on watching the kitchen, the sound of the shot stunned her. It hadn't come from the sides at all. The gunman had fired through the wall directly in front of them. This bullet tore through the window to her right, shattering glass everywhere. Even though they could have easily been cut by the flying shards, the shot hadn't come close to hitting them. That meant the shooter had fired a blind shot with the hopes that he'd get lucky.

"I can't just shoot into the wall," Griff whispered. "This idiot might have one of the ranch hands with him."

Mercy, she hadn't thought of that, and it was a good thing she hadn't sent a bullet or two his way. It could have maybe been a deadly mistake—and exactly what the gunman had wanted them to do.

There were more sounds. Footsteps. At first they were headed toward the kitchen, then the opposite direction. Either this idiot was playing games with them or else there were two of them. That reminder certainly didn't help tamp down the fear and adrenaline.

Rachel wanted to call out to her father, to make sure he was okay, but there was a chance their attacker didn't know Warren's and Ruby's exact location. He could use any response they might make to hone in on them and start firing. Even if the guy didn't go into the room, he could still manage to kill them with more of those blind shots.

She looked up at Griff just as he was making one of those sweeping glances around them. He was all lawman now, primed and ready for the fight. But she also saw something else in his body language.

The worry.

He was afraid for her, for their baby, and that wasn't a good thing to be feeling right now. It could cause him to lose focus.

The loss of focus didn't last long, thank goodness. That's because another shot tore through the wall, heading their way. Again, it didn't come close to hitting them, but the noise was deafening, and made it nearly impossible to tell if the shooter was on the move.

Another shot quickly followed, and this bullet took out the rest of the window. Rachel had to duck down and put her body over Thea's when the glass spewed at them.

"Are you hurt?" Griff whispered.

"No." Rachel wasn't sure that was true, but she didn't want him worrying about them right now.

That's because she heard another sound. Not footsteps this time. But she thought maybe it was a gasp, and it'd come from the family room, where Ruby and her father were. Rachel scooted up a little so she could try to see them, but the wall of the arched opening between the two rooms prevented her from doing that. It also didn't help that there was a lot of furniture in the way.

Mercy. Their attacker could use that to hide from view.

The gasping sound caught Griff's attention, too, because he pivoted in that direction. Rachel couldn't tell if he saw anything because she had to keep her focus on the kitchen in case the shooter came that way, but there was certainly some movement now in the family room.

Everything inside her was screaming for her to go help her father and Ruby, but that could be exactly what the gunman wanted her to do. Because there was no way Griff would let her go in there alone.

The shooter could use that as an opportunity to kill them both.

There was more movement. Louder this time, and it sounded as if some kind of struggle was going on. Rachel couldn't tell what, but she knew it had to be bad when Griff cursed and dropped down, pushing Thea and her closer against the hutch and the wall.

"Griff," someone said.

Her father.

His voice was weak and shaky. He definitely sounded as if he was still fighting the effects of the drug he'd been given.

"I'm sorry," Warren added a moment later.

That caused her breath to stall in her throat. Rachel glanced out, afraid of what she might see, and what she saw was her father being pushed into the dining room. There was someone behind him.

And that person had a gun to her father's head.

Griff HATED THAT it'd come to this. Hated that some thug was now holding Warren at gunpoint.

And he especially hated that he hadn't been able to stop it.

He'd seen the movement in the living room, but because of the darkness, he hadn't been able to make out who had Warren, and that's why Griff hadn't fired. When Griff had spotted the gun, he knew he had no choice but to get down or the intruder would have shot him. Then there would have been no one to protect Rachel and Thea.

"I'm sorry," Warren repeated. "I couldn't stop him."

Rachel's father could barely speak. Could barely stand, even. He was wobbling, but his attacker had his arm slung around Warren's waist and was holding him in place like a human shield.

Griff waited for the intruder to say something. He didn't; he just kept inching Warren closer. Probably so as to be in a better position to shoot them. Hell. And now they were trapped.

"What do you want?" Griff demanded. "And where's Ruby? Is she all right?"

The man didn't jump to answer, and Griff couldn't get a good look at his face. It also appeared the guy was hunching down a little. Probably to make certain that Griff wouldn't have a clean shot. If so, it was working. Worse, Griff couldn't tell if this was one of their suspects or another hired thug.

"He hit Ruby with a stun gun," Warren said. "She fell."

Which meant the woman could have hit her head or something. That was yet another reason to put an end to this, so that Griff could get Warren, Thea and Ruby to the hospital. Of course, the number one priority right now was making sure they were safe.

And they weren't.

None of them were as long as that guy had a gun pointed at Warren.

"Well?" Griff snapped. "Are you ready to tell me why the hell you're doing this?"

Griff probably should have reined in his temper to keep the anger out of that demand, but it was hard to do when this idiot was putting so many people in danger.

The man groaned, and it seemed to be from frustration. *Welcome to the club.* Griff was frustrated and furious that he had allowed Rachel and the others to be in the middle of this mess.

"I didn't mean for it to come to this," their assailant finally said. And Griff had no trouble recognizing the voice.

Brad.

The shock hit Griff hard. Even though Brad was on their suspect list, it was difficult to believe that a man he had known most of his life was now holding Warren at gunpoint. But Griff didn't have to guess why Brad was doing this. The man had clearly gone off the deep end.

Because of Rachel and him.

Rachel gasped, too, and shook her head. "Brad, you have to let my father go right now."

"I can't." The DA didn't hesitate. "Now, all of you throw down your guns. All three of you," Brad emphasized. "And you've probably already figured out that you can't call for help. I've planted some signal jammers all around the house, and I've got one on me."

Brad took out the small device from his pocket and tossed it onto the table. That explained why they couldn't get out a call. Brad had obviously planned this attack for him, to bring those. But maybe something had gone wrong for it to come down to this. Griff was betting Brad had planned on getting a clean shot at Rachel and him before now. But time was running out, since Egan or Court had probably sent someone out to check on them.

"If you argue with me about it or try to do something stupid," Brad warned, "I'll start shooting Warren. I won't kill him, but I'll hurt him."

Griff saw Rachel tense. She didn't argue, though. She tossed her gun. Thea's, too. Griff wasn't so quick to move, but he wasn't in a position to bargain. He didn't want to be unarmed, but this wasn't a bluff. Brad would indeed shoot Warren.

Griff tossed his gun onto the floor in front of them. Hopefully, though, it was still close enough for him to get to it if Brad started shooting.

"I didn't think it would come to this," Brad repeated. "I thought by now that Rachel would have seen that Griff wasn't right for her, and would have come back to me."

"That isn't going to happen. Not ever." Even

though she practically whispered that, it was obviously loud enough for Brad to hear, because he groaned again. "Do you think I could be with you after this?" she added. "You didn't only attack me. You attacked *us*. Griff, my father, Thea, Ruby and the ranch hands."

"Ruby and the ranch hands are fine," Brad snapped. "I used a stun gun on them and tied up the ranch hands. They never even saw my face."

But everyone in this room had seen it. And that meant he couldn't leave them alive. Brad was planning on killing them all.

Maybe.

"If you want to win Rachel back," Griff said, forcing himself to keep his voice calm, "then you should start by letting Warren go. Then we can sit down and talk about this."

"I'm not stupid." That was practically a shout. "I know it's too late."

"Maybe not." Even though it was a lie, Rachel also tried to sound a whole lot calmer than Griff knew she was.

"It is too late." Brad cursed her, calling her a vile name. "I saw you with Griff, you know. A month ago, when Warren got shot, I was going to check on you, to make sure you were okay. But I saw you leaving the hospital with Griff. I followed you, and you went to his place." His anger increased with every word he said. "You stayed the night with him. You slept with him."

Griff was about to lie and say that Rachel and he hadn't done that. It might save her. But then he got a glimpse of Brad's face, and knew that he must have seen Rachel and him in bed that night.

"What did you do?" Griff pressed. "Did you look through the window? Did you spy on us?"

"From a distance. I couldn't get too close to the house because I didn't want your dog barking. I knew then that I had to take a step back and figure out what to do. I had to figure out how to get Rachel back."

"And you did that by blowing up my car, by trying to kill me?" Rachel snapped.

She definitely wasn't trying to calm him down now. Instead, she was dealing with her own anger, something that Griff understood, since he wanted to rip this idiot limb from limb for what he'd put Rachel through.

This time Brad didn't jump to answer, but Griff could practically feel the man's ire turning to rage. "You let him get you pregnant." Brad's voice was low and dangerous now. "Don't bother to deny it. I know about the pregnancy test."

Griff figured that was because of Brad's spies, which were seemingly everywhere. Of course, it wasn't something Rachel and he could have kept secret for long, but Griff would have preferred a gentler way of telling his sister and Warren. Both were too drugged up to react now, but he was certain he'd get an earful from Rachel's dad.

If they made it out of this, that is.

Griff had hoped he would be able to reason with Brad, but they were well past that now. Especially since Brad had probably killed Dennis and Buddy. Well, maybe he had. There was another player in this.

"What happened to the gunman you hired?" Griff asked. "The one who shot at Rachel and me in Silver Creek? Or was that you?"

"No." Brad cursed again. "It was Dennis and Buddy who did that. I told them to set someone up, and they chose Warren. The idiots. Marlon would have been a much better choice. And no, I didn't murder Dennis. Buddy did when Dennis turned on us and tried to extort money from us."

"Buddy only did that because you gave the order to do it," Griff said.

"No!" Brad repeated. "Buddy did that all on his own, and then he tried to get me to pay up. That's when I knew I had to put a stop to him. I put a tracker on his truck, and I followed him to the hospital in San Antonio. I think he was on his way there to tell Helen and anyone else who'd listen what I had done. I knew then I had to finish this myself."

Griff shook his head. "You could have just finished it by walking away, by accepting that it wasn't going to work out with Rachel and you."

Brad groaned, the sound of a man who was in a lot of mental pain. "I could never accept that. Never. And I'm tired of talking about all of this."

Griff was tired of it, too, especially since he was never going to convince Brad that he was doing the wrong thing. Still, there were a few more questions that needed answers.

"Are Simon, Alma or Marlon helping you?" Griff asked. He didn't expect Brad to respond and was surprised when he did.

"Of course not," the DA spat. "I wouldn't trust any of them with this. But Marlon will get what's due him. He'll be the one arrested for this."

Yes, but something about that didn't make sense. "Why drug Warren and take him to Silver Creek if you weren't going to make us think he was behind this?"

"That was all Dennis and Buddy's doing. Marlon's the one they should have focused on. Never trust idiots," Brad snapped. "Now, I'm playing cleanup. At least if the CSIs find my prints here in the house, they won't think anything about it because I've come here a lot. I'm a close family friend. *Was* a close family friend," he corrected, but his voice cracked on the words.

Obviously, Brad was going to set up Marlon in

some way. For multiple counts of murder. And because of Marlon's past behavior, he would indeed be a suspect. Griff disliked Marlon, but the man didn't deserve this. Especially since Marlon's arrest would mean that Brad would go free.

If Griff didn't' do something, and fast, Brad might get away with it, too. He was the district attorney, and knew all the inner workings of the sheriff's office. He might even be able to manipulate the investigation.

But Griff wasn't going to let that happen.

No way would he let this lunatic kill Rachel and the rest of them.

Behind him, Griff felt Rachel move, and he hoped like the devil that she wasn't going to try to stand up. "So, the only person you've killed was a druggie CI who'd gone rogue," she said. "That's good. That means we can try to fix this."

Brad leaned out even farther, maybe to try to see her expression. It must not have been one he liked because he made a feral sound of outrage. "How could you have chosen Griff over me? He comes from nothing, and you let him touch you like that."

Hell. That wasn't the right thing for Brad to say to her. Griff was used to such talk, but it must have hit a nerve with Rachel because she cursed Brad.

Not good.

Because it apparently was more than the man could take. He aimed his gun at Rachel. Griff could have

sworn his life passed before his eyes when he thought
Brad might kill her.

But he didn't.

Brad didn't pull the trigger. He shoved Warren to
the side and, yelling like a crazy man, charged right
at them.

FROM THE MOMENT that Rachel had seen Brad holding her father at gunpoint, she had known it would
come down to this.

This had become a fight for their lives.

She hadn't expected Brad to get rid of his human
shield so that he could go after her, but the rage must
have gotten the better of him. Griff apparently hadn't
thought he would do that, either. Griff was already in
the process of reaching for his gun on the floor, but
had to stop when Brad plowed right into them and
smacked them against the wall.

The DA was heavily muscled and outsized Griff
by a good forty pounds, so the hit felt as if a Mack
truck had come at them. The jolt from the impact shot
through Rachel when her head collided with Thea's,
and Griff's sister cried out in pain. Rachel hoped the
woman wasn't hurt even worse than she already was.
She also hoped that they could put a stop to Brad before he tried to kill them.

After all, Brad still had hold of his gun.

As close as he was, if he pulled the trigger now he

could easily hit one of them. But why hadn't he just shot them when he was holding her father? Maybe Brad had figured that would have given Griff enough time to grab the gun and return fire. Then he would have been an easier target, since her father would have likely slumped down, leaving Brad's body exposed.

The impact of Brad slamming into him caused Griff to move farther away from his own weapon, and Rachel couldn't get to it, either. That's because Brad was now in the way. Even though he was right against them, he still managed to bring up his gun, and he bashed it against Griff's head.

The blood splattered across her face.

Griff's blood.

Sweet heaven. Now Griff was hurt. If Brad managed to knock him unconscious, he could try to beat him to death. Of course, she would do whatever it took to stop that, but she had to be careful not to get punched in the stomach. A blow like that could cause her to miscarry, and that was a risk Griff definitely wouldn't want her to take. Still, she couldn't just let him die. Not after…well, not after everything they'd been through.

Brad tried to take aim at her with the gun, but Griff latched onto his wrist, holding it with both hands. Brad could no longer shoot her, but he used his left fist to hit Griff anywhere he could reach.

Rachel glanced at her father to see if he was in any position to get one of the guns from the floor.

He wasn't.

Her dad was obviously still woozy, and was now groaning, maybe in pain. He'd taken a hard fall when Brad had pushed him, so he could perhaps be injured. After all, he was still recovering from the gunshot wound that he'd gotten just a month ago.

She couldn't think about that now, though. Not when Brad hit Griff again. Even though the blow was harder than the first one, Griff still managed to push Brad away, shoving him backward and then lunging at him. The impact sent them both sprawling into the middle of the floor.

Right on top of those guns.

Brad somehow managed to keep hold of his own weapon, and even got in another hit to Griff's head. Not good. She wasn't sure how much more of this Griff could take.

Rachel had to figure out some way to stop this.

But how?

She stood up to try to get closer to the fight so she could help. Brad must have seen her out of the corner of his eye because he quit punching Griff and turned in her direction. He brought up his gun.

Big mistake.

Rachel saw rage fire through Griff's eyes, and he rammed his elbow, hard, into Brad's shooting hand.

The DA's aim shifted to the right, but he still managed to pull the trigger.

The sound of the bullet blasted through the room. And through her. For several heart-stopping moments she thought she'd been hit, but she hadn't been. The shot tore into the china hutch right next to where she was standing.

Griff was still on the floor, but he grabbed Brad, trying to pull him back down. Cursing him, and her, Brad fought back. He was swinging his arms and fists wildly, obviously fighting for his life now. But then so were they.

Thea caught Rachel's arm, yanking her back down next to her. Just in time, because Brad fired again. He probably would have gotten off a third shot if Griff hadn't tackled him. This time, Brad didn't get the upper hand. Despite his size, Griff landed a punch on the man's jaw.

Brad's head snapped back, and he looked dazed. But that lasted only for a moment. The rage returned, and he probably would have tried to shoot her again if Griff hadn't continued to punch him.

Since Brad still wasn't giving up, Rachel scrambled across the floor to snatch up one of the guns that Griff, Thea and she had tossed there. She tried to take aim, but it would be too big of a risk for her to fire because she could hit Griff. She didn't pull the trigger.

But someone did.

Brad.

Unlike the other shots, this one was muffled. That's because the gun was between Brad and Griff.

Oh, God.

And that's when Rachel saw the blood.

Chapter Seventeen

Griff heard the sharp gasp that Rachel made, and even though he didn't want her anywhere near Brad, she came rushing toward them. He figured she was doing that because she thought he'd been shot.

And maybe he had.

It took Griff several long moments to realize that he wasn't in pain. Well, not in pain from a gunshot wound, anyway. He was hurting from where Brad had managed to punch him in the face too many times. However, the person who was in pain right now was Brad.

Groaning and cursing, Brad moved off Griff and looked down at the front of his shirt. There was blood and lots of it. In the heat of the fight, Brad had shot himself. But he was still very much alive.

Brad still had the gun, too.

And that made him even more dangerous than before. The sound that tore from his mouth didn't even seem human, and there was a wild, insane look in his eyes when his attention landed on Griff. Griff expected the man to try again to shoot him. He didn't, though.

Brad turned the gun on Rachel.

Griff's heart went to his throat, and he lunged at Brad as fast as he could move. This time he managed to wrench the gun from his hand. But it was too late. Griff heard Rachel make another sound. This time, it was a shout.

"No," she yelled. "Please, no."

It seemed like a prayer to him, and Griff was doing his own share of praying. He pinned Brad to the floor and looked at Rachel, hoping that he wouldn't see her wounded.

Or worse—dying from a lethal shot.

But he couldn't tell if she'd been hit because she turned and ran to her father. That's when Griff realized that Rachel was okay, but that Warren had been injured.

Griff couldn't go to her because he didn't want to risk letting go of Brad. The man was still very much alive, and Griff couldn't let him get away and try to go after the guns that were scattered around the room.

Thea was moaning, too, as she fought to get to her feet. Griff didn't know what she was going to do at first, but she kicked the guns away from Brad's reach and then took the jammer from the table. She bashed it against the china hutch.

Good.

Maybe now they'd be able to make a phone call.

"You'll need these," Thea said, taking a pair of plastic cuffs from her jeans pocket.

"Check on Rachel and Warren," Griff said, after he mumbled a thanks. "And try to call for an ambulance."

His sister practically stumbled across the room, a reminder that Warren wasn't the only one who needed medical attention. So did Thea. Probably Rachel, too. And Brad, of course. But at the moment Griff didn't care if the man lived or died. In fact, it took everything inside him not to kill the DA on the spot.

Brad smiled, making Griff's rage go up a notch. "Rachel will never really be yours." He kept smiling while Griff got the cuffs on him. "No way will Warren McCall let trailer trash like you be with his daughter."

Griff hadn't even been sure that Rachel was listening, but she made a sound of outrage and came back toward them. Thea was on the phone, probably with the hospital, and had her hand pressed to Warren's shoulder. The older man was definitely bleeding, but not as much as Brad.

"Brad's dying," Griff told Rachel, because she looked ready to launch herself at the man.

She stopped, dropped down to her knees beside

Griff and kissed him. "I just wanted you to know that I'm in love with you."

Maybe she'd said that as a dig to Brad, or Rachel could have just gotten caught up in the heat of the moment. Either way, Griff found himself wishing that the words were real, that she truly did feel that way.

Brad cursed them both, but they ignored him as they gazed at each other. There was plenty Griff wanted to tell her. Not in front of Brad, though. And definitely not while so many things were unsure.

"Egan and the ambulance are on the way," Thea relayed. "Someone needs to check on Ruby and the hands."

Griff certainly hadn't forgotten about them, but for a moment he'd been wrapped up in what Rachel said.

"I can go see about Ruby," Rachel volunteered, and she was already turning to go there when Griff caught her hand.

"Wait here with Thea and your dad. Warren needs you right now." Yeah, that was playing dirty pool, to use her father, but Griff didn't want her straying off in case Brad had a hired gun somewhere in the house.

Griff dragged the DA to the corner and used his belt to tie up the man's feet. Even though Brad was cuffed and injured, he was desperate enough to try to make an escape.

After all, he would be facing multiple counts of attempted murder and at least one count of murder for killing Buddy. Being a DA wouldn't help him, and in fact might work against him. Brad had to know that he could get the death penalty for his crimes.

Once Griff was sure the man was secured, he picked up his gun and made certain Rachel was across the room with Thea and her father. She was, and was currently applying pressure to Warren's bleeding shoulder.

"Keep watch," Griff told his sister. He hated to put this on her right now, but there wasn't a choice.

Griff waited until Thea nodded before he hurried into the living room. It was still dark, since the power was off, but he spotted the woman right where he'd left Warren and her earlier. She was unconscious, though, which meant Brad had maybe drugged her after he'd used a stun gun on her.

Griff lifted her to a sitting position, propping her against the wall. It was all he could do for her now, so he went to check on the ranch hands. Brad had said he'd only tied up the men, but he could have hurt them, too.

Griff hadn't taken more than a step or two before he saw movement in the foyer. Someone was by the now-opened front door. Griff took aim but didn't fire, because it could be Egan or someone who worked at the ranch.

It wasn't.

It was Marlon.

The man stayed back, peering at Griff from around the edge of the door.

"What the heck are you doing here?" Griff demanded.

"Brad." And that was all Marlon said for several moments. "He brought me here. He said you were going to kill him and then set me up to take the fall. I can't let you do that."

Hell.

That's when Griff saw the gun that Marlon was holding by the side of his leg.

Even though the man didn't have it aimed at Griff, that could change in the blink of an eye. And worse, Rachel, Thea and Warren were all still in the dining room and could be hit if shots went through the walls. However, Griff figured he was Marlon's target now.

"Put down that gun," Griff warned him. "Brad lied to you," he added, though he doubted that Marlon was going to believe it. Especially since Marlon thought the worst about Rachel and him.

He shook his head, and he didn't put down the gun.

"Griff's the one lying," Brad shouted out. "He shot me. He tried to kill me."

Until then, Griff hadn't known that the others could hear Marlon and him. But they didn't just hear them, Rachel peered out from the dining room, and she, too, had a gun.

"Get back!" Griff ordered.

But Rachel didn't move. "I'm not just going to stand here and let Marlon shoot you."

Griff was about to play dirty again and remind her of the baby, that this was too big of a risk to take, but he didn't get the chance. Marlon was lifting his weapon toward Rachel, but Griff didn't give him a chance to take aim.

He fired, sending two shots right into Marlon's chest.

The man looked down at the front of his shirt and his eyes widened. But only for a second before he dropped to the floor.

Griff cursed. Not just because Marlon had wasted his life, but also because Rachel had had to see another man die. Right in front of her. Heaven knew how long the sight of this would haunt her dreams. It would certainly haunt Griff's.

Outside, he heard the sound of a siren. Egan. It wouldn't be long now before he got there. Only a few minutes. But Griff didn't want him to walk in on another shooting, so he went to Marlon, kicked away the gun and checked to make sure the man was truly dead.

He was.

Griff shifted his attention back to Brad then. He was still alive, but was bleeding out fast. Warren was faring slightly better, thanks to Thea helping him. Rachel, however, didn't have a drop of color in her face.

She started toward Griff just as he went toward her, and when she reached him, she practically fell into his arms. "I was scared," she whispered.

Yeah, he'd been terrified. Not for himself. But because he could have easily lost her to a gunman.

Griff couldn't help himself. He kissed her. And while it wasn't one of those heated kisses that had landed them in bed before, it was a reminder that even now the attraction between them was still strong.

A reminder, too, that it might be a whole lot more than just attraction.

Griff would have asked her about her "I'm in love with you" comment, but the cruiser pulled to a stop in front of the house, and Egan came barreling out. Not one but two ambulances pulled up right behind him. Griff let go of Rachel so he could head to the front door.

Egan's face was a mask of worry and concern. "Thea said Brad tried to kill you," he began. He glanced at Marlon on the floor, but his attention zoomed to his sister.

"I'm okay," Rachel insisted.

"You've got blood on your face," he quickly pointed out.

She wiped it away, looking at her fingers when she was finished. "Griff's blood. I'm the only one who wasn't hurt. Dad, Thea and Ruby all need to go to the hospital."

"So do you," Egan insisted. "I don't care if it's your blood or not. You're getting checked out by a doctor." He gave her hand a gentle squeeze before he went to check on Warren.

"I will, but only after everyone else," she argued as her brother walked away. "There are two hands outside, tied up. They'll need to be checked, too."

"Court and Ian are circling the house now to make sure no one else is out there," Egan assured her. "They'll find the hands."

Two medics came rushing in, and Griff directed them to the corner where Ruby was still unconscious, and to the dining room. One went to Ruby, the other to Thea and Warren. Since this was going to quickly become a busy path, he took Rachel to one side of the living room.

Another medic came in and Griff pointed him in Brad's direction. That left Rachel and him standing there, and since she no longer looked steady on her feet, Griff slipped his arm around her.

"This one's dead," the medic called out, when he got to Brad.

Since Griff had known the man most of his life, he probably should have felt some sadness. He didn't. After what Brad had tried to do to Rachel, Griff was finding it hard to forgive him.

"He's dead," Rachel said, her voice a little shaky. He thought she might cry. She didn't. "At least we won't have to worry about him coming after us again. Marlon, either."

Yes, that was a big plus. No way did Griff want to go through anything like this again. There'd been enough danger for a couple lifetimes.

He glanced into the dining room, to see the medic moving from Brad to attend to Thea. The other one was still with Warren, and Egan was right by his father's side. In fact, Egan was now having a whispered conversation with him.

A conversation that caused Egan to glance back at Griff.

Hell. Warren had probably told him that Rachel was pregnant. Warren wouldn't have done that to rile Egan; he'd probably only told him so he'd make sure Rachel got some medical attention. But Egan wouldn't be pleased about it.

And that meant Griff had a decision to make.

The timing couldn't have been worse. Both Rachel and he had blood on them, and there was a dead guy just a few yards away. The law enforcement chaos was about to set in, because this was now a crime scene. Still, Griff didn't want to keep this inside him for another minute.

"You said you were in love with me," he stated, putting it out there. He only wished he'd softened his tone a little. It came out like an accusation.

Rachel stared at him. Then nodded. "And you're thinking I said that to get back at Brad."

Bingo.

"I didn't," she quickly added, before he could speak. "I wasn't talking to him when I spoke, but to you. That's because I *am* in love with you."

She paused, maybe waiting for him to respond. But Griff was going to have to gather his breath before he could do that. She had stunned him with those words.

"I know this doesn't make things perfect," she went on. Her tone wasn't soft, either. She sounded like she was in the middle of an argument. "Maybe my family will never want us to be together, but I don't care. And you shouldn't, either. You're a good man, Griff."

Again, no breath. Mercy. He'd always wanted to hear Rachel say those things, and now that he was hearing them, it felt like a miracle.

She frowned. "Now would be a good time for you to tell me how you feel about me."

Since Griff didn't trust his voice, he pulled her to him and kissed her. It was way too long and hot, considering that Egan was probably still aiming daggers at him. But Griff didn't care. He had exactly what he wanted in his arms.

He had Rachel and their baby.

Griff eased back, looked down at her, and was

pleased to see that he'd left her a little breathless, as well. "I love you," he said.

Despite everything, that caused her to smile. "Took you long enough."

"We found the hands," someone called out. It was Ian. "They're okay."

Good. That was one less thing to worry about. That worry list was way too long, and it was nice to scratch something off it.

The news must have pleased Rachel, too, because she pulled Griff back for another kiss. This one wasn't nearly as long or hot, because Egan cleared his throat and walked closer to them.

He dropped his narrowed eyes from their faces to Rachel's stomach. "It's true?" he said. "Did the test confirm you're pregnant?"

"Yes," Rachel answered. Kissed her brother on the cheek. "You'll be an uncle, and even though you're scowling right now, I predict you'll be happy about this one day. Almost as happy as I am."

Egan glanced around the crime scene and huffed. "Well, I suppose if you can be happy in the middle of all this, then I won't punch Griff for getting you pregnant."

"No, you won't punch him," Rachel agreed. "Because Griff just told me he's in love with me. That's good, since I told him I was in love with him, too."

Egan didn't exactly jump for joy, but Griff took

it as a good sign that the man didn't curse. "Fine. Because I was about to tell him that I expect him to marry you. Not immediately," Egan snarled, when Rachel made a sound of outrage. "Catch your breaths first. Get cleaned up. Kiss some more. And then you can talk about getting married."

That sounded a little like a brotherly decree.

One that Griff liked. A lot.

"Well?" he asked Rachel. "What do you think?"

She leaned in for another kiss. "Yes, to catching our breaths, getting cleaned up and kissing some more. Especially kissing."

And that's what Griff did. He kissed her, pulling her so close that her body was pressed against his.

"When we talk marriage, what do you think your answer will be?" he asked, with his mouth still against hers.

She smiled again. "Yes, of course. Always yes." She took hold of his shirt and pulled him even closer.

That robbed him of the breath he'd finally managed to regain, but Griff didn't care. He wanted Rachel far more than his breath, anyway, and he let her know that with his next kiss.

* * * * *

Look for the next book in USA TODAY
bestselling author Delores Fossen's
The Lawmen of McCall Canyon miniseries,
available in early 2019.

And don't miss the previous title in
The Lawmen of McCall Canyon series:
Cowboy Above The Law

Be sure to check out the books in her
Blue River Ranch series:
Always a Lawman
Gunfire on the Ranch
Lawman from Her Past
Roughshod Justice

All these titles are available now
from Harlequin Intrigue!

Get 4 FREE REWARDS!

We'll send you 2 FREE Books plus 2 FREE Mystery Gifts.

Harlequin® Intrigue books feature heroes and heroines that confront and survive danger while finding themselves irresistibly drawn to one another.

FREE Value Over **$20**

Chapter One

The old antique Royal typewriter clacked with each angry stroke of the keys. Shaking fingers pounded out livid words onto the old discolored paper. As the fury built, the fingers moved faster and faster until the keys all tangled together in a metal knot that lay suspended over the paper.

With a curse of frustration, the metal arms were tugged apart and the sound of the typewriter resumed in the small room. Angry words burst across the page, some letters darker than others as the keystrokes hit like a hammer. Other letters appeared lighter, some dropping down a half line as the fingers slipped from the worn keys. A bell sounded at the end of each line as the carriage was returned with a clang, until the paper was ripped from the typewriter.

Read in a cold, dark rage, the paper was folded hurriedly, the edges uneven, and stuffed into the envelope already addressed in the black typewritten letters:

Author TJ St. Clair
Whitehorse, Montana

The stamp slapped on, the envelope sealed, the fingers still shaking with expectation for when the novelist opened it. The fan rose and smiled. Wouldn't Ms. St. Clair, aka Tessa Jane Clementine, love this one.

***

TJ St. Clair hated conference calls. Especially this conference call.

"I know it's tough with your book coming out before Christmas," said Rachel the marketing coordinator, her voice sounding hollow on speakerphone in TJ's small New York City apartment.

"But I don't have to tell you how important it is to do as much promo as you can this week to get those sales where you want them," Sherry from Publicity and Events added.

TJ held her head and said nothing for a moment. "I'm going home for the holidays to be with my sisters, who I haven't seen in months." She started to say she knew how important promoting her book was, but in truth she often questioned if a lot of the events really made that much difference—let alone all the social media. If readers spent as much time as TJ had to on social media, she questioned how they could have time to read books.

"It's the threatening letters you've been getting, isn't it?" her agent Clara said.

She glanced toward the window, hating to admit that the letters had more than spooked her. "That is definitely part of it. They have been getting more…detailed and more threatening."

"I'm so sorry, TJ," Clara said and everyone added in words of sympathy.

"You've spoken to the police?" her editor, Dan French, asked.

"There is nothing they can do until…until the fan acts on the threats. That's another reason I want to go to Montana."

For a few beats there was silence. "All right. I can speak to Marketing," Dan said. "We'll do what we can from this end."

Don't miss
Rogue Gunslinger *by B.J. Daniels,*
available October 2018 wherever
Harlequin® Intrigue books and ebooks are sold.

www.Harlequin.com

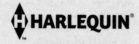